COASTAL VOICES AND VISIONS

Published by St. Petersburg Press
St. Petersburg, FL
www.stpetersburgpress.com

Design and composition by St. Petersburg Press
Cover design by St. Petersburg Press and Amy J Cianci

Paperback ISBN: 978-1-964239-06-4
eBook ISBN: 978-1-964239-07-1

First Edition

COASTAL VOICES AND VISIONS

Contents

Contents

INTRODUCTION

Coastal Voices and Visions is a collection of short stories, essays, and original photographs of coastal communities where people love to live, work and visit. Like the tides, coastal voices and visions ebb and flow through this collection.

Follow secret paths into forbidden gardens where families fuss and help each other. That support shows up in many ways—plummeting to retrieve a lost flip flop, steeping medicinal teas, returning a lost treasure, even rescuing people in a listing boat during a storm.

Paddle down sunlit rivers in a tipsy canoe. Kayak across a deep channel beside a dolphin that leads you to the sailboat where a handsome sailor welcomes you aboard. The sea lures her tribe with intriguing offers. Be transported to and from islands once navigated by ferrymen. The captain's tales of island history, tradition, and culture were as plentiful and salty as hidden mangrove tunnels.

Embrace the gently rocking Gulf of Mexico and playful surf of the Atlantic Ocean. Florida settings include: Cedar Key's Old Florida charm, splendid sunsets and full moons rising over Pass-a-Grille and Redington beaches, Juniper Springs' glassy waters, beach music and munchies at the Blueberry Patch in Gulfport. Solve the mysteries in a time-travel story set at The Tides Hotel and Bath Club, a historical fiction featuring a cameo vision of a famous couple. Some stories introduce distant coastal communities like Kiawah

Island in South Carolina and visions of the Mediterranean Sea that a young boy sees only in his dreams.

Curated by Suzanne Norman, Carlene Cobb, and Doris Norrito, the imaginative works compiled in *Coastal Voices and Visions* express optimism to overcome odds. Swim, stroll and sail into each story's surprising twists, inviting readers to ponder new possibilities.

Nine authors contributed to this collection, which is divided into two sections: Short Stories and Essays. Both sections include original photography. All storytellers have crafted a variety of tales, peeling back the layers of coastal lifestyles forever salted by the sea and her sister waterways. Find your favorite spot to read and enjoy these coastal adventures.

Short Stories:
- **Suzanne Norman**—Lady Blue and Carolina Undercurrent
- **Carlene Cobb** — Cottage 15 and Seaside Gardener
- **Doris F. Norrito** — Papa, What Is the Sea?

Essays:
- **Barbara Sartor** — First the Ferry, Then the Skyway
- **Henry E. Sorenson, Jr.** — Canoeing with Mom on the Juniper Springs Run
- **Rick Rhodes** — Bootprints from Yesteryear
- **Joan Girard Baptist** — Peace of the Park
- **Kendel Ohlrogge** — A Nostalgic Night at the Blueberry Patch
- **Louise S. Harris** — Coastal History at Weedon Island Preserve

We dedicate this collection to Doris F. Norrito, our treasured writer friend, who was always ready for a "Coming Up Roses" adventure.

SHORT STORIES

I must go down to the seas again, for the call of the
running tide
Is a wild call and a clear call that may not be denied.

JOHN MASEFIELD, SEA-FEVER

Lady Blue

BY SUZANNE NORMAN
Three Rooker Key, Florida

The Gulf was the color of a blue margarita, the kind with curaçao added for a tropical vibe. Lani lifted the paddle and smoothly brushed the water at an angle, moving the yellow kayak over the surface in a rhythmic motion as dolphins swam by. A radiant sun and an island one hour away helped her leave loneliness onshore and feel a sense of adventure. The opalescent sands of Three Rooker Key, along with a dozen boats anchored there, became visible as she paddled closer.

Was Marc here yet? He'd called last night to see if she'd join him on a sail this morning. Her independent streak and need for a daily fix of exercise prompted her to kayak out, promising him a rendezvous. This was their third date...if you could call it that. She'd had doubts about the men she'd met in Florida so far, yet his easygoing style didn't seem prone to deception like the others. His thirty-foot sailboat, Lady Blue, rocked slowly in the island's eastern cove. Gliding closer, she shouted "Ahoy, captain."

"Well, if this isn't a sailor's dream come true. Lani, glad you made it."

"With all this sun and glassy water, I'd be a fool to stay home. I'm a California girl at heart, but I'm warming up to

Florida more. Especially when a handsome man offers a free lunch."

"Free and easy. . .grab the line and I'll tie it off."

She ran the line through the cleat on the kayak and lifted herself onto the sailboat's stern.

"Welcome aboard. I'll get you a drink."

"Sounds great," she said, pulling off her tee shirt to reveal a bikini top.

The Gulf of Mexico seemed calm and easy compared to the crashing Pacific. After thirty-five years of California life and the 2021 pandemic closures, she had transferred to the Tampa office when the environmental engineer opening became available. Florida's environmental problems lacked the urgency of earthquakes, faults and mud slides. Packing up and driving across country spurred her energy.

Since her arrival in Tampa, the surrounding coastline had been a natural haven of discovery. She'd been meaning to join a kayak club, that is, until she met him on the marine construction project. His muscular build, six-foot three height and rugged chiseled face combined with a sailor's soulful eyes made her comfortable at once, reminding her of her father.

"Here's something cold."

"Thanks. That was a good workout. Glad I left early. Heard the winds may pick up this afternoon."

"A godsend for sailors. In the meantime, I've got this little motor that will kick butt and get me in, though I believe it's slower than your kayak."

It probably is, she thought.

"Marc, how much of the Gulf coast have you explored?"

"Mostly from Anclote Key down to Siesta Key and Sarasota. I've lived here six years and never become bored. These islands are as beautiful now as the first day I saw them. Maybe even more so."

"What do the weather forecasters say here. . .just another perfect day in paradise? I'd have to agree."

"Lani, you're fast on that kayak. It's not as easy as it looks. I took one sea kayak trip. Seems I was in over my head."

"Thanks. Years of practice in the Pacific along with a persistent father taught me how to handle one. He's an adventure writer, you know, a true outdoorsman."

"Syms. Not the Outsider magazine writer Jeff Syms?"

"Yes. You've read his work?"

"I followed his south Pacific series last year. What a guy."

"Yes, he's something. My mother is exceptional too. She's a genetic engineer and very adventurous as well. She just doesn't get to sail away as often. Anyway, I'm blessed to have such a family. I miss them. They'll visit this fall, I think."

"I'm impressed. By the way, I like your blonde hair pulled back like that. It accents your face and brown eyes."

"Sick of those old business suits, huh? I am too. The sun feels greats. I get a warm glow inside."

"I know what you mean. Let me get the food together. Relax awhile."

"I will." She walked forward to the bow and found a good spot to spread the beach towel. Hot sunbeams relaxed her body while the faint strains of a classic Joni Mitchell tune pulsed through the cabin hatch. She loved the *Blue* album.

Maybe he's a big fan, like she was. She wondered if that's why he named the boat Lady Blue.

In the distance, clouds gathered in an anvil shape. Thunder boomed.

Ten minutes later, Marc came on deck with a feast: cold steamed shrimp, cheese and crackers, strawberries, and chilled white wine.

"I heard thunder. Damn, I hope it bypasses us," he said.

She walked to the stern and sat. "Now this is a picnic. You outdid yourself Marc." This guy has class—even has real wine glasses, not disposable cups.

They peeled shrimp, then dipped them into a tangy sauce.

"Toast to the captain. Long live sailors."

"Hear, hear!" Thunder interrupted Marc. Toward the west a vortex had formed, a waterspout of gray green cloud-filled wind funneled over the water.

"Over there . . . isn't that amazing? If we were in Kansas, I'd be running for the nearest cellar."

He grabbed his phone to check the weather app and turned on the marine weather radio. The weather broadcaster didn't say a word about waterspouts, just a chance of rain and thunderstorms.

"Lani, help me fasten some more lines to the dinghy and kayak."

"Okay." The wind had picked up considerably in the last few minutes as Marc checked the sails, hatches and anchor line.

"Go below. I'll join you in a minute."

"Yes captain," she said lightheartedly, although she felt a serious situation brewing. She'd been on enough boats to know that worried look. He knew the Gulf weather better than she did. Rain began falling. Thick heavy pellets battered the boat with fierce intensity. Marc ducked in the cabin and shut the hatch behind him.

"We'll have to wait it out. Usually, these squalls pass quickly. Hold on." A roaring sound reverberated throughout the sailboat.

Lani gripped the wooden seat and cushion. Swaying up and down, the boat held its anchor in the maelstrom. Marc slipped, lost his hold and fell on her.

"Are you all right?"

"Stay still," she said. His hard body felt safe on her.

"I'll move." The winds whipped the boat up and down like a play toy. He hit his head, and sat beside her, extending his arm around her for stability. She pictured the funnel cloud in her mind, trying to visualize the height and width. Anything to stop her body chemistry from feeling the urges. Her heart said go for it; her brain said no. She put her arm around his body, kissing his lips and sending her tongue exploring into his mouth. He responded with a tight embrace and leaned backward, bringing her down on top of him.

"Slowly," she whispered, kissing him. She felt very connected. Heavy rain pummeled the boat as the wind abruptly ended.

"Marc, did you hear that?"

"What?"

"The wind stopped."

"Who cares? I've wanted to hold you this way since I first met you."

"You did?"

"Wasn't it obvious?"

"Well, I know the chemistry was there." She giggled.

A serene quiet and a gull's call signaled the end of the rain. The cabin was hot and sticky. Lani got up, grabbed his tee shirt and opened the hatch to a shining sun. A neighboring sailboat had overturned. Her kayak was there but the dinghy was missing.

"Marc, come look."

He stood up and looked out. "Let's get over there and help."

She knew he'd be that kind of guy.

Sailboat on the coast of Dunedin, Florida

Photo: Suzanne Norman

Carolina Undercurrent

BY SUZANNE NORMAN
Charleston, South Carolina

April 1974

I sink my feet in the sand, listening to the repetitious sound of dancing waves washing the shore, leaving seafoam and shells in its crescendo.

My daydream is interrupted by the noisy Friday afternoon bustle of doctors and interns outside my office. It reminds me that tomorrow I'll be on Kiawah Island with my friends.

"You still here? Time to go, Ally."

"Thanks Dr. Vonn, have a good weekend."

I grab my shoulder bag from the drawer and pull my long hair in a ponytail. The rhythms of my workday are over, and I'm eager for some fresh air. I walk quickly to the elevator before another task comes my way.

"Have a good weekend, Ally," says an intern that I flirt with often. Who am I kidding? These interns are too busy learning the art of medicine to think about dating.

"You too, Eric" I reply, flashing a smile at him before stepping into the elevator down to the afternoon breeze.

I unlock my bike and pedal away from the university hospital for the short ride home, inhaling the fragrant honeysuckle. All's well until the rain starts on the last stretch of Meeting Street to my apartment. It's my Ally Earhart luck; my own Murphy's Law. Most days I enjoy biking around Charleston. Despite today's downpour, the April air holds the warm breath of spring.

I lift the wet bike inside the stairwell area and climb the three flights of stairs to my apartment. There's a small paper bag at my door containing my lost seashell bracelet, last seen at my neighbor Lynn's house. A note inside the bag said she'd found it in her car. *Thank you, Lynn. It was handmade by my artist friend* I thought as I unlock the door.

After showering and changing into dry clothes, I open a beer and put my Linda Ronstadt *Different Drum* album on the turntable. Stretching my body on the worn sofa feels good. I like my clerical job at the hospital though wages are paltry. My mantra is to live for the weekends and outdoor Lowcountry gatherings. The ringing telephone ends my reverie.

"Hi Ally," Johnny says.

"Hey Johnny. What's happening?"

"Are you coming to the beach at Kiawah Island tomorrow? College is on spring break. Wes got the key. Julie's going too."

"Yes, I can't wait."

"Julie will make sandwiches at Wes's house so meet us there. Weather's gonna be windy."

"Cool. I'm in."

Any day with Johnny is an adventure. He's my childhood

friend, a tall blonde known for his surfing skills. Some days I wish he was more than a friend. Julie is Johnny's petite blonde girlfriend who drives the horse carriages as a Charleston tour guide. Wes and Johnny are in college because it's better than the draft call for Vietnam. We're a band of 19-year-old beach lovers, and freedom from rules is a dream day.

Kiawah Island is a wild place where few venture as it's behind a locked metal gate. The island world is owned exclusively by the C.C. Royal family, lumber barons from Georgia. Eighteen families with money or political clout have beach cottages. Wes's family is in that category.

Just last month, a local TV reporter announced the Royals had a sale pending to a Kuwaiti firm who would develop the island. I thought *this might be our last hurrah on Kiawah.*

The next morning, I dress in jeans, a peasant shirt, boat shoes and a hat, then stop at the Piggly Wiggly to buy colas and potato chips. A few blocks further, I step onto the porch at Wes's house and give a familiar hug to my friends. We fill the old blue Ford truck with all we need for a fun day: friends, a cooler of sandwiches and beer, a ratty beach blanket, and a yellow Lab named Hunter in the truck bed.

We cram into the truck's bench seat and roll down the windows. I squeeze in next to muscular Wes as we leave downtown, heading south on the narrow tree-lined road bordered by tomato farmlands and the giant Angel Oak. Van Morrison's "Tupelo Honey" plays on the radio.

At the end of the paved road, the truck bumps down the dirt path to the gate. Wes unlocks it, grumbling "Glad it opened, it's rusty." He's a fairly quiet guy, a thinker. He would return to college upstate after the break. Although I like him, he's not around enough for me to date. As he drives, the bouncing continues along the rough path until we stop at the forest's edge. We ease out of the truck, unload Hunter and our picnic goodies. Suddenly, we hear loud scuffling in the forest.

"It's a wild boar stamping around, looking for food. Move it," Wes says, tightening his hold on Hunter's leash. The dog tries to dash into the forest after the boar, but Wes wins that challenge.

We walk quickly for a few minutes, distancing ourselves from the woods. Passing the sand dunes bordered with sea oats, we carry supplies to a wide swath of packed sand at the tide line.

"This looks like a good spot," I say. We spread the blanket, anchoring it with the cooler.

"I'm lighting a joint, need it after seeing that hog," Johnny says, passing the slim marijuana joint to share as we sat down.

We talk and laugh as the shorebirds caw. The sound of the waves is our music. Offshore, shrimp boats trawl for the daily catch in the rolling waves of the Atlantic. The dark blue water glistens in the sunlight.

"Let's walk to the point," Wes says. "Shells are better there at low tide." A big white weathered house, the Vanderhorst place, becomes visible in the distance.

"Off to find the seashell treasures. Come on Hunter," Julie replies.

On this windy spring day, we amble about a half-mile on

the deserted beach to the point where the ocean meets the Kiawah River. I fill the shell bag with whelks, cockle shells, and shark-eye moon shells.

Johnny calls out, "Dolphins at 1 o'clock. That's a good luck sign." We watch as a pair of dolphins surface and swim past us at the point.

As we stroll along the beach, my hat blows off into the cold water. Hunter trounces in the water immediately and retrieves it. He's a smart Lab.

"Good boy," Julie says as she runs on the beach with him. After a few minutes, Hunter stops near the water and begins to dig frantically.

Julie shouts, "Come see what Hunter found. It's shiny."

We walk over and see a piece of a seaweed-covered driftwood with something attached glinting in the sun.

"Find something to dig with," Johnny says as he moves Hunter aside. We find a few large cockle shells nearby and dig deeper.

"Wow, look at this," I say as Wes and I pull up the driftwood, uncovering a thick gold chain with a large cross.

Wes examines it, scraping wet sand off with his fingernail. "There's an inscription on the back of the cross: Davis B. Don't think it's been in the ocean too long. It's not tarnished."

Johnny adds, "Remember that bad storm last month? A shrimper drowned off Seabrook Island. Seems his name was David or something like that."

Since I work at the hospital, I remember the accident; the man had a wife and child. Normally, our group avoids the police and Coast Guard. Johnny was recently stopped for speeding, and police searched the car for marijuana, to no avail thankfully. He's on their radar for his long-haired surfer looks. None of us want jail time for smoking a little marijuana here and there.

"You're right" I say. "I remember seeing the forms at the hospital after the accident. Want to sell it and split the money or return it to the shrimper's wife? My friend Katie works in medical records and can find the wife's address."

"I say sell it. I could sure use some extra cash," Julie says.

"Forget the cash, Julie," Johnny replies.

"Let's not mess it up at a pawn shop. My dad knows all the pawn shop owners since he was a prosecutor. He'd disown me," Wes says. "Besides, it's worth finding out if it belonged to the man."

"So, I assume we agree to try and find the wife?" I ask.

"I guess," Julie whines as the guys nod-in agreement.

The winds still for a moment as the sun rises higher. We return to our blanket and enjoy our picnic lunch of egg salad, potato chips, and beer. I stow the cross and gold chain in my beach bag to take home.

~ ~ ~

Once we return to town, I think *how can I approach Katie for this task? It might cross the gray line in the records department.* I take a deep breath and dial her number.

"Hello," says Katie.

"Hi. I need a favor."

"What's up?"

"It's confidential."

"What the hell is this favor?"

"Remember the shrimper who drowned last month? I know you saw the records that week. All I need is the name and address of the shrimper's wife."

"Hmm. As long as the records are still in our files and haven't gone to the medical examiner's office. I'll let you know Monday. Otherwise, you're out of luck. And you'll owe me a beer."

"Thanks so much. See you Monday at work."

I hope she finds the records. The Coast Guard ship that found the shrimper that weekend was docked at the base eight blocks from the hospital. Protocol is to transport the body to the nearest morgue. That's why the hospital has records. I didn't want to ask the medical examiner since police or the Coast Guard would wonder why I was snooping.

On Monday, I share the story with Katie, showing her the gold chain and cross that I stashed in a small velvet jewelry box.

"I understand why you want to pursue this," Katie says. "And it's lucky I worked my magic and found the records. It was in the stack to go to the examiner's office. Swear you won't use my name...I could get in trouble."

"I swear. Thank you. I promise I'll let you know what happens."

Davis Bolen is the drowned shrimper's name. His wife

Angela and their son live near Shem Creek in Mount Pleasant where the shrimp boat fleet docks.

Since I don't have a car, Johnny agrees to drive me to Mount Pleasant Tuesday after work. It's a short drive north from Charleston, over the Cooper River. We decide not to call the wife first but to scout out the house. We pass Shem Creek and the shrimp trawlers docked outside the seafood restaurants.

"Turn here. It's in the old village section, 305 Platt Street," I say.

"Should be three blocks down," he says.

There's a car in the driveway of a weathered frame home with a long front porch so he parks on the street.

"I'm going to the door and see if Angela is home," I say.

"I'm coming with you."

I held the velvet box with the cross and chain close to my side as he knocked on the door.

"Who is it?" a woman's voice says tersely.

"Ally Earhart, Mrs. Bolen. I found something of yours."

She opens the door.

Johnny says, "We found this on the beach at Kiawah last week, tangled on a piece of driftwood. So sorry about your husband."

I hand her the velvet box. "I'm sorry about your husband."

She opens it and gasps. "Oh, I can't believe it," as tears flow from her eyes. "I had this monogrammed for Davis last year. This means so much. I'll give it to our son when he's older. Thank you, uh, your names, again?"

In the background, we hear a boy say "What's wrong Mommy?"

"It's ok," she calls to the boy and then turns to face us.

"Ally Earhart and Johnny Ward," I reply with a forced smile as a few tears wet my cheek.

"Thank you for bringing the cross to me. You made my day. How did you find me?"

"Through a friend of the crew. We thought you'd want it. Good night, Mrs. Bolen" says Johnny. She nods and closes the door.

We walk to the car and he drives in silence until the stop sign before Shem Creek Road.

"I think we need a shrimp dinner," he says.

"If you buy," I add.

"Okay."

"We'll toast to another rewarding day at Kiawah. I'll miss it if the developers close it."

"Me too. Times are changing here."

A bit of sadness comes over me as I sigh, *yes, they are.*

~ ~ ~

April 2021

The letter arrives from a post office box on John's Island, near Kiawah. I open it and unfold *The Post and Courier* newspaper article entitled "Kiawah Island Mansion fetches record $20.5 M". The clipping is about the Vanderhorst Mansion, a fully renovated historic home. The two-story house sits on 16 ½ acres at the edge of the Kiawah River. The buyer was an estate LLC, the original owner's family name. Did they buy it back?

A yellow sticky note on the back of the clipping reads *'Know you'd remember this place. Come to Charleston and stay on my restored sailboat. A Morgan 36'. It's docked on the river. Wes.'*

Maybe it's time to return to Kiawah. The drive from my north Florida home is five hours. His wife passed away two years ago; my husband four summers ago. Boating soothes the soul. It also challenges you to use your skills in ever-changing weather. I could use a little extraordinary excitement, away from Florida. Sea fever always runs strong.

S.C. Lowcountry Moss-Draped Oaks

Photo: Suzanne Norman

Sunset over North Redington Beach

Photo: Carlene Cobb

Cottage 15

BY CARLENE COBB
North Redington Beach, Florida

"Kai!"

She recognized his voice in the distance. Turning away from the Gulf of Mexico, she shaded her eyes and searched the white sand beach for her husband, Luke. She spotted him waving his arm overhead, maybe 100 yards away. In response, she opened her arms wide and twirled in a circle, while breaking waves splashed over her bare feet. Kai felt her smile open and grow as she walked toward him, watching his every step.

With both hands tucked into the pockets of his khaki shorts, his polo shirt flattered his athletic physique. His strides elongated as he quickened his pace, showing leg muscles toned by years of biking, surfing and playing drums. Kai loved the way he moved. As they got closer, she saw his half-smile dimple one side of his face, an expression of boyish nonchalance that she knew well and found charming. Married five years now, she was as excited to see him as she was when they met seven years ago. Her busy schedule of fact finding, interviewing, and taking photos out of town the past week did not stop her missing him.

"Hey, you! How'd you get here so fast?" Kai asked.

"Left work a little early today. Couldn't wait to see you."

"I missed you, too." She slid her right hand up the inside of his left arm, pausing to caress his rounded bicep. She felt him tense the muscle and remembered telling him why women really take a man's arm when they're walking together. "It's not about needing help to stay balanced. It's all about how good it feels to hold on to this," she recalled confessing with a playful squeeze. She wondered if he remembered that first confession.

Not wanting to waste a moment of their North Redington Beach getaway, Kai was eager to plunge into the Gulf for a swim before sunset. Send all her deadline worries and family stress floating away, out to sea. She and Luke summarized their week apart as they strolled.

"So, which beach on this press trip was your favorite?" Luke asked.

"Hmm, you know I love St. Augustine. The ocean, the history, the vintage downtown full of art galleries, music, cafes and happenings. But I don't want to be there in hurricane season with the floods and busted up A1A Highway. The ocean seems more powerful, but the Gulf has its gentle greatness, too. Our hometown beaches, from Honeymoon Island to Pass-A-Grille and Fort DeSoto Park, are gorgeous and offer magnificent sunsets. Every beach has its own charm."

"So, you haven't decided on your favorite?"

"Depends on what you want to do," Kai replied. "You need waves to surf, but our Gulf is better for swimming — and other things. You'll have to wait and read the story."

Luke reported highlights of the wit and grit flowing from the newsroom, spicing his stories with satiric one-liners. She enjoyed his sense of humor and the laughter they shared. Grateful for the easy banter between them, it was a welcomed break from the mounting family pressures and work stress that had recently turned them into what she called "the Bickersons."

She closed her eyes and took a deep breath. In her mind she saw her spirit animal, a sleek dolphin shimmering silver in the sunlight as it breached the sea's surface. That image reminded her of the power in staying positive.

Just as she thought she had pushed aside her trouble-in-Paradise concerns, Luke disrupted her vision, asking the dreaded question.

"Did you schedule that appointment with the specialist?"

"No." Her decisive one-word response was intended to put a full stop to that conversation.

"No? No what?"

"Ah, you're pressing. OK, Luke. No, I did not make the appointment with the doc your sister recommended."

"Are you going to?"

"If I need to, I will. Right now I do not need to because there is nothing wrong with our fertility. Five years married. No baby. So what? I will schedule a medical consult if and when I need to, and you will be the first to know. I love your sister, but she is not in charge of our life. The only healing we need right now is a swim in the Gulf. Coming with?"

"Sure." Luke's voice sounded like he was not so sure. He pushed the key card in the slot, the lock clicked, and he pushed the door open to a whole new conversation.

"Wow! Nice place," Kai gushed, sweetening the mood. "Oh, and beautiful flowers. And what's this? Champagne? And chocolate-covered strawberries? Luke, did *you* do all this?"

"Well, I ordered all this. You know, only God can make a strawberry."

"And only *you* can open the champagne. Please. I've never acquired the skill. Unless you want to save it for later?"

Luke popped the cork while Kai gathered glasses and opened the curtains to let in the light. The Gulf view always calmed her.

"Here's to a sweet swim, an amazing sunset and a great getaway at one of our fav beach joints," Luke said, raising his glass.

"And, to a wondrous weekend," Kai said, "filled with very little work and a whole lotta' love."

"Hear, Hear!" Luke said as they clinked their glasses. He added, "With a nod to the Led Zeppelin classic."

Champagne-steeped kisses followed until Kai challenged, "I'll beat you to the water."

"In your dreams!"

Kai stood up, reached down and pulled her dress over her head, tossing it on the sofa. She was already wearing her bikini under the dress. "Wanna' bet?"

"Trickster!" Luke said, grabbing his swim trunks.

Dashing out the door, Kai called over her shoulder, "Last one in the water is a big, fat otter!"

Then she was gone.

Kai trotted toward the sea with the wind sifting through her hair. Luke joined her at the tucked-away alcove down the beach where she had led them for a more private swim and sunset viewing. The rocky, mangrove-covered grotto was barely visible and rarely visited by tourists or locals. She liked it for that reason. She knew it was safe to swim there and watch the sunset as long as they left the grotto before the high tide rushed in. Luke walked past her and stood in water up to his chest.

"You know, you are not actually in the water. *This* is in the water." He dove into the next passing wave and vanished. Kai followed his path into cooler, darker depths. When he surfaced, she flashed a coy smile as rippling waves caressed her shoulders.

"Don't feel bad about being last in the water," he taunted. "Otters look cute in the water."

"Otters are cute," she said, wrapping her arms around him, "but not as handsome as you."

Beneath the blanket of waves that covered all but their heads and shoulders, Kai wrapped her legs around Luke's hips. He slid his arms down her back and gasped. "Kaimana! You're bottomless."

She laughed and showed him her bikini bottom scrunched into a ball in her right hand. "I'll cover up before we get out. Bottomless feels good in the water."

"Yeah, oh yeah, it feels good, but..."

"Come on. The Gulf will rock us gently like babies in a cradle. Remember how good it feels?"

"Yeah, I recall my awkward sprint to the shore a few years ago when I had to go get your towel to wrap around you so you could get out of the water without being arrested."

Laughing, Kai squeezed tighter and pressed against him while untying the drawstring to loosen his trunks "Ah yes, lovely Washington Oaks Park with the gold coquina decorating the beach. Surf was up and knocked that thing right out of my hand. But that won't happen here. This. Is why the Gulf. Is better. For lovers."

Once they were skin on skin below the sea's surface, there was no stopping their passion. Their bodies rocked together with the waves' rhythm. Looking down on them from the painted sky above, seagulls circled and shrieked.

"Hear the seagulls laughing?" Kai said breathlessly. "They're happy for us."

But her heart suddenly thumped with a different cadence as she considered that the gulls' cries may not be laughter, but a warning. Sensing sundown's feeding time closing in, she knew they needed to unfurl, part their joined loins, slip back into their swimsuits and head for shore.

"We better go in," she said, looking out at the horizon. She pushed back from Luke, floating backward as she slipped into her bikini bottom. "Ready?" she asked.

"Yeah, ready. Oh, *shit*! What was *that*?" Luke shouted before launching into a race-paced free style stroke. "Let's go!" he shouted. "Get to shore!"

"What *is* it?" Kai shouted.

They both stretched out to swim to shore. Luke shot ahead then circled back to position himself behind Kai, who swam as fast as she could. Then she felt a bump from the side and another against the back of her leg and screamed, "*No!* No! What *is* it?"

No reply. All she could hear was her own heart pounding. "Luke?"

"I see it!" he shouted. "Keep going!"

"Shark?" Kai yelled. When Luke did not answer, she turned to look for him. Thinking he may have submerged, she peered into the water in a desperate search.

"Luke, where are you?" Between the waves, she saw a gray streak darting toward her. She felt another bump and gasped. "Oh God! I think it's a dolphin! Luke, where are you?"

Finally, he popped up so she could see his head and shoulders bobbing in the rising tide. He waved her toward the beach again. Just then, the dolphin breached for air, circled back, submerged then bumped her again, forcing her into the onshore plunging waves. The dolphin's boost also pushed her closer to Luke's arm reaching for her.

"Look, there she goes." Kai pointed to the curved, gray fin just before the dolphin surfaced again for air. Then it turned back toward deeper water.

"Yeah, looks like a dolphin; keep going," Luke commanded, giving Kai's hand a strong tug, pulling her through the lacey shallows. They stood and paused for a moment to catch their breaths before splashing through the last swirling watery steps before reaching the silver shore.

"She came to get us out of the water before the shark found us." Kai said, panting to catch her breath.

Luke didn't speak or let go of Kai's hand until they reached the first patch of dry sand. They both dropped there as the red sun began to melt into the horizon.

"Wow, some sunset, eh, Caballero?"

Luke shook his head, looking down between his feet. Salt water dripped from his dark curls and off the tip of his nose. "Never been so glad to park my ass on dry sand. But yes, Baby. Before some sea creature started shoving us out of the water, it was a delicious sunset in the water with you."

Kai snuggled up against his side. "You swim fast when you want to."

"Want to? Needed to. I've seen dolphins come in close to shore before, but this is the first time I've ever been thumped by one."

"Well, this is their home," she murmured. "They let us visit until it's time for us to go."

"Kai, if you tell this story, delete the part about our bottomless escapade in the sea."

"Aw man, that's the best part."

Luke turned to her with a serious gaze. She studied his hard-focused eyes, eyes that enclosed the oceans.

"Of course. You're right. That part of the story is just for us. Deal?"

"Deal. I'm glad you said it was the best part. Never had to

compete with a dolphin for top billing. Not sure which was more exciting for you."

"Ah, Caballero. You know you are always the best and most exciting part of everything—including dolphin encounters."

"So, new topic," Luke declared. "Tell me again why your hippie parents named you, Kaimana." Surprised he wanted to hear that story at this particular moment, Kai took a deep breath and began.

"Well, you know my parents love the sea, and you know they are a couple of old hippies. When they were younger hippies with a baby on the way, they researched names and chose Kaimana because it means powerful sea.

"They wanted to empower you?"

"Maybe, at least they wanted me to know the power of the sea and nature in general. Since they did not want to know the gender until I was born, they chose the gender-free shortened version of the name, Kai."

"And do you feel the power of the sea?" Luke asked.

She turned to him with her coquettish smile. "Yes. Didn't you?"

He replied with a kiss. The afterglow lit up the sky with pink, coral, lavender and that shade of aqua that shows up sometimes after the green flash sparks at the horizon when the sun melts into the sea.

"So beautiful," Kai said.

Luke pulled her close again. "Yes, beautiful. And the afterglow in the sky is nice, too."

Kai started laughing and couldn't stop. Luke looked at her,

surprised. She shrugged. "Nerves?"

He stood and offered his hand to assist her rising to her feet in the soft sand. "Want to go rescue that bottle of champagne and figure out some dinner?"

~ ~ ~

Their second champagne toast of the day included a brief mention of gratitude for the dolphin and the magnificent sunset they shared. Luke ordered food while Kai showered, slipped into a new sun dress, styled her hair into long, swirling waves and applied fresh lipstick. Luke opened the door for the dinner delivery and closed the drapes on the dark night outside. Kai lit candles and they chatted through dinner like the best of old friends.

"What did you think of the Museum of History?" Luke asked.

"Loved it! What a great resource. So much information, amazing vintage photos, artifacts and mystery-solving documents. Oddly, I became super intrigued by the Joe DiMaggio exhibit featuring visuals of the Marilyn Monroe love story: photos, news clippings, even autographed baseballs."

"Didn't know you were a baseball or Marilyn Monroe fan," Luke said.

"I wasn't. Didn't know much about either, but I learned. Benefit of being a low-paid freelance correspondent—being assigned to stories that lead you to experiencing new things."

"Absolutely," Luke agreed, refilling their glasses.

"The Monroe / DiMaggio love story is part of St. Petersburg history because they stayed at the Old Tides Hotel and Bath Club in its heyday in the 60s. DiMaggio was in St. Pete serving as a batting coach with the New York Yankees during spring training. Anyway, I did some more research online and found additional photos of them walking on the beach, relaxing in a cabana, they looked happy. Alas, soon after that stay at the Tides, their love story came to a tragic end."

"Yeah, not a happy ending," said Luke. "Where was the Tides, again?"

"Here. Well, I mean near here. On this same beach. The property was sold in the 90s and the whole thing was demolished. The new version of the Tides is timeshare condos. Totally different."

"Different how?"

"I must have told you my parents and their friends stayed at the old Tides in the 80s and up until it was sold and destroyed in the 90s. They always planned ahead to rent the same space, cottage 15. I'm told I was there too, but I was a baby and don't remember it."

"Wait, really? They remembered the room number?"

"Oh, cottage 15 wasn't just any room. According to my mom, it was 'the best beach cottage in all the land.' She talked about it like she was reading me a fairy tale. Apparently, cottage 15 had a fireplace, a Gulf view bay window and front porch on the beach, full kitchen, attached garage, it was all the way down at the end of the Tides complex, very private.

But wait, there's more." Kai tapped her empty glass against the champagne bottle and Luke refilled her glass.

"Promise you will never tell my mom I told you this."

Luke shrugged and nodded.

"OK, in a rare moment of T.M.I., my mom disclosed to me that the old Tides' cottage 15 is where I was conceived."

"What? No way!"

"Yes, way. She's quite sure of it. She journals everything and keeps track of details most people don't. She and my dad stayed there to celebrate their birthdays on October 28. She said it was a watercolor weekend, raining more than usual. So, they were inside more than usual. Nine months later I was born on the 29th of July, a Leo lioness."

"Wow! Do mothers tell their daughters stuff like that?"

"Mine does. Swear to me, you will never tell her I told you. She didn't tell me it was a family secret but may have meant the information just for me."

"I swear," Luke held up his right hand. "Trust me, that is not a conversation I want to have with your mother. I don't think I've heard these stories about cottage 15 with a fireplace. Seems too hot here to ever need to light a fire."

"I don't know. Maybe the weather was not as hot back then. You know that climate change thing? Anyway, I'm babbling on and on, sorry. I'm kind of jazzed. It's not every day I get thumped by a dolphin."

"OK, so that dolphin could be your spirit animal, as you say, but I cannot confirm or deny any shark sighting in the vicinity," Luke said, using his TV-lawyer voice.

"Did you want to see a shark?"

"Hell no!"

"No, me neither. So, we got our wish. But just because we didn't see the shark doesn't mean it wasn't there, swimming low in deep water, preparing to... *attack!*" Kai grabbed Luke's forearm with both her hands, pressing her nails into his skin to simulate a shark bite.

"Hey! Objection. Speculation." Luke pushed her hands away. "Glad you don't do those fake nails anymore or you might have drawn blood." They both laughed. Kai wished this dolphin moment would never end.

"I missed talking with you," she said, "among other things. So, how about no more story assignments that take of us away for a whole week or more? Unless we can both go."

"Deal. Where do I sign?"

"Ha! I'll show you after I clear away the dishes."

They quickly tossed containers in the waste basket and wiped down surfaces. Kai turned on the water and reached for the dish soap, but Luke reached for her hand and lifted it to his lips.

"Leave it," he said.

And then they were kissing and caressing each other again. "Wait," said Kai. She pulled away to light more candles until the entire room pulsed with flickering candlelight. They fell together on the bed, tossing clothing aside like leaves caught in the wind.

Kai pounced on top of her husband, positioning herself like an odalisque painting, sitting upright, straddling his pelvis. Her dark auburn hair spilled artfully over her bare shoulders, breasts and back, curving like scrollwork just above her waistline. Suddenly, she saw something from the corner of her eye and gasped. She turned to look behind her through the flickering light and saw a couple standing outside a window.

"Huh?" Kai sucked in a breath, unable to speak or think of anything but covering her bare breasts with her hands. A blonde woman and a tall, dark-haired man, stood arm-in-arm outside the window, looking in at her and smiling.

She grabbed the bed linens and yanked them up around her before turning back for another look. The woman at the window flashed an open smile then pulled the man's arm as they both slid back into the shadows of the dark beach outside.

Kai swallowed hard and croaked, "Luke! Someone's at the window. Looking in at us!"

"What?"

She fell forward on his chest, breathless. "I know I locked that door. Did you leave the curtains open?"

"What? No. Kai, what is the matter? Do you want me to get up and check it out?"

"No. No. Don't move. Keep everything right where it is. Let's just trade places, okay? Just roll with me, baby. I want you on top, yeah?" She pressed her legs tight against him and together they rolled to the left to change their position.

"Did you read a new chapter in the Kama Sutra for this maneuver?" he asked, between panting and moaning.

"Nah, we don't need the Kama Sutra," Kai spoke just above a whisper. "We're writing our own book. Now the peepers outside the window can only see your nice, strong back and I'll stay out of sight down here. You don't mind, do you?"

"Nah, we'll never see 'em again. Baby, if anybody got a look at you up there with the firelight in your hair, on your skin... My God, that's an image they'll never forget. I'll never forget it. You are so beautiful."

"Thank you," was all she could say between breaths. She thanked him for not telling her she was crazy, for not jumping up to show her that nobody was there watching them, for continuing to love her even in those moments when nothing made sense. She thought she heard the sound of a crackling fire near the corner of the room and recalled Luke mentioning firelight, not candlelight, but she could not speak of it in that moment.

"Better now?" Luke asked. You okay?"

"Yes, Baby. Yes, I'm good. Soooo good. Yes..."

And so, the night unfolded, manifesting their toast from earlier that day with "a whole lot of love."

Kai woke with the dawn, feeling sated and dazed. She watched her husband sleep while she sat silently with her thoughts about the amazing night they had shared. She looked around the room for clues about what happened, or seemed to happen, the night before.

The candles had burned down to their tiny black wicks. She vaguely remembered Luke getting up to extinguish them all. She slipped into her dress and tiptoed around the room.

She checked the door and sliders. She peeked behind the closed curtains and even felt the walls, not knowing why. All appeared secure and private with closed drapes covering the sliding doors. How did she see people at a window where there was no window. Was she dreaming? Hallucinating? Seeing ghosts? Was she crazy?

When she peeked again behind the heavy drapes, something red in the far corner caught her eye. She pulled the curtain's hem aside and bent down for a closer look. There on the floor was a fresh red rose. When she picked it up, two velvety petals slipped through her fingers. She watched them flutter to the floor and land together beside a baseball. Kai's jaw fell open and confusion flooded her mind.

She scooped the baseball and fallen rose petals and quickly tucked them into her backpack. Her mind raced, thinking the baseball must have been left behind by a former guest and missed by housekeeping staff. The rose was fresh. Perhaps it dropped from the arrangement Luke ordered for the room. She strained her brain to make sense of it all, but the puzzle parts did not quite fit. Quietly, she made a cup of herb tea for herself and brewed a pot of coffee for Luke.

Sipping her tea, she noticed the distinct smell of burnt firewood. Scanning the room in a full 360 turn, she realized the smoky scent was in her hair. She pulled a handful forward to her face and inhaled deeply. Yep, firewood. In that scary moment when she saw a couple watching her from a non-existent window, she also remembered catching a glimpse in her peripheral vision of a crackling fireplace with flames licking stacked logs. Yet, there was no fireplace and no bay window open to the waterfront view in this room.

Kai put the rose in a tall glass to separate it from the other flowers in the vase, having no idea why that felt important to her. She had read about quantum physics, time's relativity, and those who claimed to be "travelers." She had always regarded the notion as an intriguing but impossible fantasy, like Tinkerbell and Peter Pan in *Neverland*. It happened in books and films, not in real life. However, she knew of no evidence confirming whether or not time travel might be possible. All she knew was for a few fleeting moments, she and Luke somehow seemed to be making love beside a fireplace in the old Tides' cottage 15, part of a building that was razed in 1996. She wondered if something impossible could, at the same time, be the only plausible explanation. Could the unreal magically become real?

"Good morning," Luke said from the rumpled bed.

Kai brought him a cup of coffee. Her abdomen felt different, but not in a way she could describe. She felt certain there was new life in her body, but she chose to keep that feeling to herself and wait for pregnancy test results. To stabilize the peace with Luke and his family, she offered him a promise she believed she would never have to keep.

"Baby, I promise I'll make an appointment with that specialist in a few weeks after I get these stories done. And I'll let you know when it is scheduled. OK?"

Luke nodded, stretched, yawned and reached for his coffee cup. Kai relaxed, too. She understood that sometimes a woman just knows what she knows, without proof.

Closing her eyes, Kai welcomed her spirit animal into her thoughts. She felt a strong surge of power and a bubbling-over sense of joy. She chose to trust the magic of unproven possibilities—the power of nature that her hippie parents named her to embody. She would wait, knowing the evidence would come to the surface for air when the time was right.

Luke leaned close to her and asked about the smoky smell in her hair. She shrugged and mentioned the candles. He looked doubtful. She knew he could distinguish the strong aroma of fireplace smoke from the delicate fragrance wafting from a dozen votives. Since she knew not the source of the smoke tangled in her hair, she simply smiled and shrugged again.

Concluding that Luke's reporter's curiosity was piqued, Kai intended to divert his sleuthing to a more pleasurable mystery. Hearing the sound of a light rain tapping the roof, they both looked up at the ceiling and then at each other.

"Sounds like a watercolor morning," she said, reaching for him. "I'm craving an avocado and soft-boiled egg for breakfast, but I don't want to go anywhere. Can we relax here and order from the hotel restaurant?" she asked sliding her hand up his thigh.

Luke nodded and his face dimpled on one side with that charming half smile she adored.

"I'm, uh, putty in your hands, Powerful Sea."

"Ah, Caballero, I'd say you're more like solid gold."

No Vacancies during Tides Heyday

Photo: Donna Parsons Renck

Seaside Garden Cottage

Photo: Carlene Cobb

Seaside Gardener

BY CARLENE COBB
Pass-a-Grille, Florida

A fresh sea breeze added a whisper of salt to the scents of rosemary, basil, and lemon verbena. Hearty plants and vibrant blooms fluttered as the wind rustled through Aunt Vi's lush garden. The distinct sound of a cardinal's song piped from above, and Aunt Vi's rocker stilled. Turning away from the stale stories, told over and over at every family gathering, Aunt Vi looked up toward high branches shading what she called her garden of delights. Stretching her arm up, like a conductor, she signaled her command for quiet, and the chatter on the front porch hushed. She leaned forward in her chair, searching the tangle of greenery and blooms for the songbird. Then she pointed toward some arcing limbs, heavy with clustered, purple berries. The slender stalks bobbed above the birdbath.

"Look! There she is in the beautyberry," Aunt Vi spoke just above a whisper.

A female cardinal flew down, landing on the edge of the birdbath. Her male companion patrolled above her in an elliptical pattern. When a squawking blue jay approached, the scarlet guardian darted into its path, diverting the intruder nearly twice his size. The female dipped her beak into the water. She splashed into the basin for a quick dip before ascending into seclusion among the branches.

Some chuckles and chatter resumed until Aunt Vi raised her arm again, this time extending her index finger. A warning. She pressed her finger to her lips and shot one of her intense glares in the direction of some raucous laughter from the corner of the porch. That's when the male cardinal dove and splashed down into the bird bath, flapped his wings and shimmied from beak to tailfeathers, sending an iridescent spray of droplets all around him.

After his flamboyant display, he preened his feathers, paused and cocked his head appearing to stare directly at Aunt Vi. "Hello, handsome," Aunt Vi said softly. The bird tipped his head from side to side before his swift exit into a vanishing point among the sea grapes. Aunt Vi laughed and resumed her rhythmic rocking.

Watching, awestruck, sixteen-year-old Natalie O'Malley's gasp turned into laughter. "Wow! that's so cool," she said from her vantage point on the top porch step. There she had a clear view of the garden and could also watch the guests come over to greet Aunt Vi with birthday wishes. She noticed how her great aunt's blue eyes twinkled and the lines around them crinkled when she smiled and welcomed each guest. Everybody called her Aunt Vi, related or not.

Natalie's mother flashed her movie-star smile, saying, "When cardinals appear, angels are near. How nice of the cardinals and angels to grace us all with their presence on your birthday celebration, Aunt Vi."

"Oh, they visit regularly," Aunt Vi answered. "Last week

they showed their two babies where the bath and bird feeders are in the garden..."

Suddenly, the screen door banged, interrupting Aunt Vi's story. Natalie turned to seek the source of the noise. It was her older sister Madelyn, and Cousin Earl, up to their usual rude, rowdy antics. Hooking their arms together, they started singing "We're off to see the wizard. The wizard that lives at the beach!" With linked arms, they staggered across the porch.

Aunt Vi's rocker stopped again. Her smile flat-lined. "Hey, now," she called to them. "You two don't go strolling down the primrose path too far. It's just about supper time. We're dining early so we have time for a sunset stroll after dessert."

Earl took a sharp turn and walked back to face Aunt Vi. Natalie looked at Earl then turned to search for her parents on the porch. They had gone inside. Earl stepped close to Aunt Vi's rocker and bent over so his sneering face was so close to her, their noses were nearly touching. Madelyn stepped back from Earl.

"Don't worry Auntie. We won't scare away any of your little bird friends."

"See that you don't."

"Or what? You going to poison me with some of your twig tea?"

Aunt Vi sat up straight in her rocker, glaring at Earl. Then she stood tall with her arms akimbo, just staring, unflinching. In that moment, Natalie imagined Aunt Vi might just take a bite out of Earl's nose and spit it out on the ground, like she would the bruised side of a peach. She never did, though. Old Aunt Vi just glared and stood her ground until Earl stepped back and staggered away. He reached for his flask, took another swig and turned toward the steps where he stumbled over Natalie.

"Watch it, you klutz," she shouted, scooting out of his way.

"Sorry, Natty-Batty," said Earl. "Didn't see you there. Hey, where's your boyfriend, anyway?"

"Well, anyway, Early-Burly, why don't you call me Nattie or Natalie, like everyone else does?"

"You just always looked like a Natty-Batty to me." Earl shrugged, adding. "You know, Maddy loves a paddy and Natty's gone batty," he chanted and laughed at his own joke. Then he repeated his question about the boyfriend's whereabouts.

"Who wants to know?" Natalie replied

Maddy leaned into the chat to add her follow-up query, "Me. I wanna' know. So, where *is* Sean? Haven't seen that handsome rascal in a while, not even in church last week."

"So?"

"So, where's he been?" her big sister demanded.

"And that would be your business because—?"

"Uh, because I want to know."

"Ask *him*." Natalie regretted her words as soon as they slipped out.

"Maybe I will." She hooked Earl's arm again and pulled him into another awkward stumble down the porch steps. As they crossed the lawn in quicker strides toward the beach path, Earl pulled his phone from his front pocket.

"Yeah, like he really wants to talk to you and Earl," Natalie yelled at their backs.

"Or *you*?" Her sister shot over her shoulder. Then she smiled and said, "We won't be long, Aunt Vi. I'll pick some flowers for the supper table."

"*Pashaw!* Plenty of flowers right here in the garden," Aunt Vi muttered under her breath.

Aromas of a rosemary-wrapped standing rib roast, cinnamon-sprinkled sweet potatoes, and fresh-from-the-garden collard greens beckoned the family inside to check on the food and refill their glasses. Aunt Vi seemed relaxed in her rocker, making it squeak high then low with the soft tap of her foot to keep it going in between.

From her top-step perch, Natalie squinted in the afternoon sunlight and wondered what Aunt Vi looked like when she was young and pretty, before her lined skin draped over her high cheekbones and taut jaws. Natalie closed her eyes and tilted her head back. Feeling the wind on her face and sifting through her hair, she thought of Sean's admiring touch and the sound of his voice when he said softly, *"your hair is like spun gold."* Chasing away that mental film clip, she opened her eyes again and noticed Aunt Vi tipping her head back to catch the breeze, too. Nearby weeping willow branches nodded while wind chimes tinkled and bonged from low branches.

The birthday celebration of the mysterious Aunt Vi was in full swing with feast preparations in the kitchen. Natalie knew she should be in there helping, but she felt compelled to stay outside. She pulled her blonde hair back into a ponytail, took a deep breath and released an audible sigh. She liked breathing in the familiar scents like rosemary, basil and lemon verbena, but she was most curious about those unfamiliar, pungent odors, spiking her senses with a bitter edge. Natalie decided she needed to know Aunt Vi's gardening secrets.

She started learning by counting the earth boxes and trying to identify the herbs and vegetables she recognized. The boxes stretched halfway around the house to the back steps leading to the kitchen door. Each box housed an overflowing bounty of greens, some with blooms she recognized, like Thai basil, chamomile and mint. The paths between the boxes were overgrown with wild grasses, vines, and wild beach sunflowers. The garden appeared healthy and productive but overgrown and in need of some weeding and pruning.

"You seem pensive, Natalie," Aunt Vi said. "Something on your mind?"

"No ma'am. Nothing special. Just enjoying the fresh air – though I do wonder how you keep up this big garden all by yourself. We got a little garden at home, and it's a lot of work for the four of us."

"Yes it 'tis a lot of work but being in the garden and growing food is so satisfying for me. Of course, I can always use a little help. Anytime you're not too busy with school, come on over. Gotta' get an early morning start. Get out there before it's too hot."

Natalie smiled, "I just do some weeding and pruning in our garden at home. Mom picks out the plants. And we just started with the herb garden over spring break. I don't know much about growing veggies and herbs. You think you could teach me?"

"You're smart. Honors classes and all, I understand you're getting a jump on college courses in your senior year, right? You'll be a quick study. My mother and grandmother taught me most of what I know about gardening. You know, some of the best knowledge is passed down mother to mother, woman to woman. And I have some good reference books, too. You can read any of them anytime you like."

"OK," Natalie was a bit surprised to hear herself saying. "I'll help you in the garden—and read some of those books, too."

Aunt Vi motioned toward the front door. "Better go in now and see about dinner."

"Yeah, it smells great and I'm hungry as a bear." Natalie wanted to ask her aunt about the strong-smelling plants, but her hunger outweighed her curiosity at that moment. She decided to bring it up while they worked in the garden together, and she would make that happen as soon as possible.

"Where is your sister?" her mother asked.

"Went for a walk on the beach, I believe," answered Aunt Vi. "Now, don't be cross with the kids, Winsome. Who can blame them for wanting to stay outside on such a lovely day? And, your Natalie says she wants to help me in the garden. Isn't that nice of her?"

Natalie smiled because everyone called her mother Winnie, but when Aunt Vi wanted to make a point, she used only proper names. Her mother looked surprised for a second before flashing her Hollywood grin and putting her arm around her daughter's shoulders. "My little Nattie? Yeah, she's a good kid. And smart."

Natalie tried to hide it, but she always blushed when her mother and father bragged about her high grades. It felt good to know they were proud of her.

"Yep," Aunt Vi said. "Smart, pretty and helpful. She's the whole package, as they say. Just like you, Winsome. You know, that is the perfect name for you."

"Well, thank you. My dad chose the name. It's a family name, after his grandmother."

"I never knew that," said Aunt Vi. "Your dad must have been an intuitive man."

"Yes, he was very wise and loved figuring out how to fix things."

"And, you know what?" Aunt Vi continued as she basted the roast. "I've been wanting to extend the garden to that shady patch under the oaks out front. I sure could use some help preparing the beds for that expansion."

Aunt Vi and Winnie bustled about the kitchen and dining room. Natalie realized this gardening project had taken on a life of its own, and there was no way she would be able to get out of grubbing in the dirt with old Aunt Vi now. She kept her goal in mind—garden secrets.

Aunt Vi insisted they sit and enjoy dinner while it's hot, rather than waiting for Earl and Maddy to return. She extended her arms, palms up, in an invitation to join hands around the table before saying her traditional blessing.

"Thank you, God, for this day. Thank you for our work and

play. Thank you for the birds that sing. Thank you, God, for everything."

Hands squeezed and glasses clinked to kick off the meal. As serving bowls were passed, Natalie hoped nobody noticed her appetite, as she scooped second helpings. "These collards are delicious, Aunt Vi. Are they from your garden?"

"Yes, they are, so there's plenty. And, we have dessert. Save some room, everyone."

"Sorry, sorry guys," Earl burst through the front door and began telling his tale. "Maddy and I took the wrong trail and got a little lost. Walked way past the beach access. It looks different after the storms. Not like I remember it. Different."

Maddy chimed in, adding her personal brand of drama, while she arranged her freshly plucked posies in a vase. Natalie watched her parents' concerned gazes lock briefly before they let the tension melt.

"How 'bout some cake and coffee?" Aunt Vi said as she stood and turned toward the kitchen without waiting for an answer. She returned with her traditional birthday cake, a homemade pineapple upside down cake, which she insisted she make for herself with fresh pineapples from her garden. Three candles flickered from the center pineapple ring. The family sang the happy birthday song, and Aunt Vi made her silent wish and blew out the candles. Natalie followed her into the kitchen to help.

"Sorry, Aunt Vi, your cake looks delicious, but I definitely did *not* save any room for dessert; in fact, my belly feels stuffed."

"How about a cup of ginger tea?"

"Oh, no, please don't bother."

"No bother, I want some, too. Hand me that jar that says Ginger/Hibiscus on the middle shelf there in the pantry," Aunt Vi set the kettle on the stove, and Natalie stepped into the pantry and started reading mason jar labels. Pushed way in the back on the shelf nearest the floor, she noticed jars with labels she had never heard of before: *Pennyroyal, Mugwort, Queen Anne's Lace, Dong Quai, Angelica, Black Cohosh...*

"Did you find it?"

Natalie grabbed a jar in the middle of the top shelf and read the label aloud.

"Hibiscus/Ginger/Licorice/Peppermint. This one?"

"Perfect."

The stuff inside that jar looked like chopped roots, weeds, grasses, seeds, and blood-red crumpled flowers. Natalie thought drinking tea made from flowers seemed like a nice idea, but she wondered how something called mugwort would taste. Ever curious, she grabbed her phone, returned to the pantry, and clicked off several photos of the labeled jars on the bottom shelf. She peeked out and nobody was in the kitchen. She heard the piano from the living room. A sing-along had begun. Natalie stepped back further into a dark corner of the pantry and tapped out a search on her phone. With great interest and intention to continue more in-depth research later, she captured the following information:

"Emmenagogues are abortive herbs... most effective before a pregnancy reaches six weeks. You might have some in your kitchen

or garden right now: parsley, mugwort, pennyroyal, Queen Anne's lace seeds, Angelica/Dong Quai and black cohosh all have abortive properties... For centuries before institutionalized health care, women managed their reproductive health using plants like these... These herbs have a good chance of bringing on your cycle."

The tea kettle whistled. Natalie met Aunt Vi at the kitchen island and watched her set the kettle down and pick through the herbs, scoop several teaspoons in the tea diffuser and pour the water over the tea. "Remember, only boil the water, not the herbs."

"Mmmm. Smells nice. What looks like wood chips?"

"Ginger root and licorice root both have a woody look. Both aid digestion, among other things, and licorice root is a natural, healthy sweetener. Let it steep six or seven minutes, then we'll have a cup of tea before we clean up."

Aunt Vi returned to the guests gathered around the piano, and Maddy joined her sister in the kitchen with more plates for the dishwasher.

"We called your boyfriend," she said, "but he didn't answer. So, we left a rather insistent message on his voicemail."

"You know, you could just mind your own business and leave him alone."

Maddy poked her elbow into her sister's left rib. "And what fun would that be? Hey, what smells so good?"

"Tea. It's steeping."

"What kind of tea?"

"Custom blend Aunt Vi made."

"Oh, custom blend, huh? Does it contain an eye of newt?" Maddy lowered her voice to just above a whisper. "Li'l sis, some folks say Aunt Vi is a wise woman." Maddy gestured air quotes with her hands. Natalie returned a blank stare as Maddy continued. "You know, the politically correct term for a witch?"

"Yes, I know what some stupid people say. And I know she's just a gardener who likes to grow vegetables and herbs to eat and drink. I'm pretty sure you know that, too."

"Quite a gifted gardener, I'd say, growing all this stuff in beach sand," Maddy said, "Have you seen that monstrous garden in the back? It's a jungle. I heard there's more wise women around here. They say they're healers."

"If *they* did a little research, they would figure out that earth boxes allow gardeners to adjust and control the soil, so the vegetables are not growing in beach sand. And who are *they*, anyway?"

"Friends, trusted sources. But here's what you should do," Maddy pressed, "wouldn't it be fun to find out—you know, if she really is like a wi..."

"All right, ladies," Aunt Vi startled the whispering sisters with her stealth return to the kitchen. "Who is loading the dishwasher and who is helping me put food away?"

During the cleanup, Natalie and her great aunt watched each other. Natalie felt certain that they each had a secret they preferred to keep hidden. When their eyes met, they both smiled. Natalie wondered if their secrets could be something they both need to know but were afraid to share. The quiet tension in the kitchen fueled a fast cleanup, and Maddy hurried out to return to the sing along.

Natalie felt relieved when her sister left the room without mentioning Sean again. She and Aunt Vi sipped their tea, and she felt its flavorful warmth helping her relax. Then she heard her own voice again asking if she could spend the night there to get an early start on the garden in the morning. "Like you said, gotta get out there before it gets too hot."

"Yes!" Aunt Vi said, clapping her hands together. "We'll get an early start!"

Natalie's parents were not as thrilled with the idea, Winnie's eyes showed her concern. She mentioned "church tomorrow" and "final exams coming up."

Aunt Vi skillfully negotiated past every obstacle, right down to agreeing to a 3 p.m. pick-up on Sunday, so Natalie would still have time for studies at home. Rarely did anyone in the family win a debate against Aunt Vi. She pretty much called the shots. In the end, Winnie gave Natalie a hug and agreed to a 4 p.m. pickup time the next day. Somehow an extra hour got added to the deal.

When Aunt Vi shared some of her plans for the garden project as everyone stood on the front porch saying good-bye, Maddy rolled her eyes. Her obsession with Sean's absence would have to wait. That secret was safe for the moment because Maddy had other discoveries in her mind. She pulled her sister aside and whispered close to her ear, "Nattie, find out if she's a witch."

Natalie and Aunt Vi waved from the porch as cars pulled

away from the house. Then Aunt Vi showed Natalie her room and everything she would need.

"Can we make it to the beach for sunset?" Natalie asked.

"I think so. I'll bring a thermos of tea."

"Oh, what kind? You have a lot of different teas."

"All herbs, no caffeine—except some of the green teas. Actually, there's still a whole pot of hibiscus/ginger and that's good hot or cold. Shall I bring that?"

"Sure. How did you learn so much about growing herbs?"

"I was always fascinated with how plants just spring up from the earth to help us heal."

"Help heal what?"

"Everyone needs a little help healing something every now and then. Pharmaceuticals are made from plants, you know."

"So, you're saying there's an herb growing in the ground for every ailment?"

"Well, I can't say every ailment, but many. Plants and what we extract from the right plants, help us heal, energize, relax, feel good, be our best. Ready for sunset?"

"Yes, I am ready. Love to see sunset at Pass-a-Grille beach. And I want to read the books you have about growing herbs, too. I'm curious about that one I saw in the pantry called mugwort. That's a weird name. What does that do and what does it taste like?"

Aunt Vi gathered a few things into a beach bag, they slipped into flip flops and left the kitchen. Then she answered the question.

"Mugwort *is* a weird name. It tastes rather earthy, similar to some of the mushroom teas. I like to combine herbs for their benefits and their flavors. So, mugwort and pennyroyal, black cohosh and others have properties that helped me and my sisters in our younger years with irregular, painful moon time, as we called it, you know, menstrual cycles. I got in the habit of keeping a supply of those herbs that help resolve that kind of discomfort."

"And the teas help?"

"Yes, they do."

"How?"

"Well, Nattie, there is a lot to this subject. The short answer is certain herbs can be used to stimulate the blood flow when your cycle is delayed. So, everything gets back to normal, and you feel like yourself again. I cook with herbs and make tea with them. And some plants I grow just for the butterflies and birds—beautyberry and firebush for the birds, milkweed for the monarchs, rue for the swallowtails. Rue has a strong, bitter aroma. It grows well, like a weed."

"Maybe that's what I smelled in the garden. It's for butterflies?"

Aunt Vi nodded and smiled. "Yes, swallowtails love rue. We may see some in the garden tomorrow, and maybe some monarchs on the milkweed. We will have some sweet dream tea when we get back if you want a nightcap."

"Sure."

They walked the oyster shell path through a wooded area and then another path to the narrow road with a crossing for the beach.

"Yay, we made it to sunset, Aunt Vi, and it's a great one! Did you order it for your birthday?"

"If that were possible, I would order it every day. And tonight's a double feature. It's also a full moon. Do you want to watch it rise?"

When they neared the beach and heard the gentle waves lapping against the jetty, Natalie felt like the waves were taking the sting of her heartbreak out to sea.

"Aw it's a beautiful night, Aunt Vi! You're so lucky to live right here by the beach. Do you walk over here a lot?"

"I do. I walk here every day I can. I love the sound of the waves and seagulls and kids laughing. Kids are always laughing at the beach. They just naturally understand its wonder."

Walking in the shallows and watching the fiery sunset, Natalie began to feel relaxed for the first time in weeks. Except for the aching desire for Sean to be there with her instead of old Aunt Vi, she felt hopeful for new possibilities.

"Just two gals, one young, one old, both loving the sunset and waiting for the moon to shine down on the Gulf of Mexico," said Aunt Vi. "Beautiful!"

They walked out on the jetty, sat on a couple of flat rocks, and watched the sunset colors ignite the sky as the big red sun melted into the rippling waves. The afterglow stretched across the sky in pastel ribbons of light.

"The sea breeze feels nice on my skin," Natalie said. "And it feels good to walk off that big dinner I ate."

"You sure you want to wait for the moonrise?"

"Yes, I do. Unless you're tired."

"Not a'tall. Watching the moonrise energizes me."

They watched and waited for the moon to rise, letting waves splash over their feet as they walked, laughing about the shells being Mother Nature's pedicure. Natalie felt the wet sand being sucked from under her feet and suddenly felt dizzy. She grabbed Aunt Vi's arm to steady herself.

"You OK?"

"Yeah, just lost my balance for a second there."

Aunt Vi pulled a blanket from the beach bag and spread it on the soft sand. Then she handed Natalie a piece of cake on a plate, saying, "Wait, don't eat it yet."

She pushed a candle into the center of a pineapple ring. "Your turn to make a wish. It doesn't have to be your birthday to make a wish. You can make a wish on the full moon." She lit the candle and Natalie closed her eyes.

"Let me think. OK I have a wish."

"Don't tell me, just go ahead and wish."

Natalie took another deep breath, pressed the palms of her hands together and wished for the same thing she had been wishing for weeks: *Bleed. Bleed. Bleed.* She blew out the candle.

"OK. So, Nattie, I don't go looking for problems to solve, you know? But you've been asking a lot of questions, and I've shared a tiny bit of information about how herbs can be healing. Do you know that I have helped people use herbal therapies for all kinds of health challenges, from headaches, anxiety, digestive issues and infertility, to name a few?"

"No, I did not know that."

"Well, that is not common knowledge for good reasons, especially now. But I share it with you because today I noticed that you looked so worried. You look better, happier, here at the beach."

Natalie smiled, but tears were building.

"I am just a gardener, but I may be able to help you feel better if you tell me what is troubling you. 'To thine own self be true.' You've heard that quote, right?"

"Yes, Aunt Vi. Shakespeare's, Hamlet, right?"

"See how smart you are? Will you take a few deep breaths with me for clarity about what concerns you and what you want?"

Natalie nodded and Aunt Vi took hold of her hands.

"I'm going to inhale, taking a deep, cleansing breath, filling my lungs then holding the breath at the top just until it feels like my breath may pop out of the top of my head. Then I exhale slowly, with a vocal sound, something like a sigh but more purposeful. I'll do the same thing two more times. Will you do that with me?"

Natalie nodded. They began to breathe together. After the third exhale, Aunt Vi said softly, "To thine own self be true." Clarity. Clarity. Clarity."

Natalie's voice shook as she spoke through her tears.

"I can't have what I want."

"Why not?"

"Because Sean said we'd get married, but now he's backing out. He wants me to go to a clinic out of state somewhere, anywhere there's a legal abortion clinic. He said he'll pay for it. I'm not interested in forcing him to marry me, and the last thing my parents need is another mouth to feed. Besides, I don't want to embarrass my family. Adoption is an altruistic choice, but I know I can't do that. Again, I don't want to embarrass my family. I just want things to return to normal. Go to my classes, go to my job, finish college, maybe Sean and I can get back together. Who knows? When I found the information about herbal abortions online, I thought it sounded like a simple solution to just drink some tea and everything goes back to normal."

They both looked up to see clouds passing over the huge yellow moon rising above the palms.

"Well, my dear, I have all kinds of herbs to help with all kinds of situations. I will help you any way I can, but going back is not possible. Life only goes forward, not backward."

"It seems like this country has gone backward."

"Good point. It breaks my heart after all our work in the 70s to get laws passed to protect women's reproductive rights. It's hard to believe this war on women is happening now. I can make your tea, but you cannot tell a soul that I helped you with this project—for your protection and mine."

"I understand that. I'd never rat you out, Aunt Vi."

"Looks like your generation will have to carry the torch for women's rights now. We thought we got the laws passed and it was done, but no. Poof! Our rights vanished. So, maybe you'll help to fix that, my dear. Meanwhile, I'll make tea."

"Yes, Aunt Vi. I promise. I'll work on that after I graduate high school, OK?"

They watched the moon rise and cast its light on the dark, hungry sea.

"Natalie. I believe every woman has a right to choose what care she needs and what happens to her body and to her life," said Aunt Vi. "There is no judgment here. But now with these crazy new laws, you must be especially careful, very smart about it and very safe. And, most important, you must be very sure about what you want. Not what someone else wants you to do, right? I can and will support you in any decision you make. So will your parents, by the way. Your mother is like a tiger when it comes to her girls. And don't tell your sister I said so, but your mom is especially proud of you. You are her rock star. Again, any herbal therapies I discuss with you for whatever reason must be our secret. Again, for your protection and mine."

"Yes. I promise. I don't feel much like anyone's rock star right now. Just stupid."

"Nevertheless, you are your parents' rock star. Mine too."

Natalie wiped away more tears.

"Shall we go make some sweet dream tea?" Aunt Vi asked, offering her hand to help Natalie stand up in the soft sand.

They turned together toward the path. As they neared Aunt Vi's garden, its fragrance welcomed them. Natalie took another deep breath and hummed a deep sigh, comforted by knowing Aunt Vi was now in her corner. She no longer wrestled with this agonizing decision alone.

"You know, Aunt Vi, what would be such a sweet dream?"

Aunt Vi wrapped her arm around Natalie's shoulders and waited for her to continue.

"Me, you and baby puttering in your garden between my Bio Chem classes—someday."

"Absolutely. A very sweet dream. A perfect dream. When you're ready. Someday. Maybe soon. Maybe later. When the time is right, we'll all grow together."

Full Moon over Gulf

Photo: Carlene Cobb

Sea Dreams

Photo: Carlene Cobb

Papa, What Is The Sea?

BY DORIS F. NORRITO
Jerusalem

"Papa, what is the sea? I hear you and Mama talk about the sea but with such a happy sadness. Tell me why the sea makes you happy and sad together?"

Giorgio looked with hard gentleness at his young son, wondering how to explain the whirlwind of life changes that occurred since his boy's birth eight years ago that now forbids him to know the sea. He shook his head as if trying to dislodge the jumble of thoughts that eluded answers. Straightening his collar he looked directly at the boy.

"When you're older, son you will understand," he stated firmly knowing the usual dismissal would not do and that neither annoyance nor calm would stop the boy's insistent pestering for a reason. Each question reset a past cursed with untenable answers layered with guilt. Staring with helpless pleading into his son's searching eyes, he listened patiently as the boy spoke.

"I see tears and I want to know why Mama cries then you both laugh when you remember the sea."

Giorgio sighed deeply. "Memories can be happy and sad," he said, drawing his son close with a reassuring hug. "Later, my son, later; later I'll explain," he falsely assured.

The curious child searched his father's faraway look and thought: *later never comes;* and left without an answer, imagination filled the void.

"Tell me about the sea Papa, is it far?" Sea: when spoken the word set pictures in his young mind: endless water unlike anything known in his inland world, water covering all space, hiding all the land, riding on treetops and wetting everything. He imagined its sound, one only such a vast sea had that spoke like a wish in a dream - *sea*, he said softly to himself, how can a soft sound make Mama's eyes tear and bring joy and pain at once?

Giorgio saw his son's faraway look and took in a deep breath. "No, it is not far," he said dismissively before suddenly snapping sharply, "but we cannot go!"

"Never?"

"Not now, not yet," he said, his eyes flaring, his voice edged with new surfaced anger he had fought to control.

His son felt as if his father had suddenly slapped his face.

Giorgio had long been haunted by his son's thirst for reason which began as soon as he was able to speak. His "why" of early childhood became pleas for reasons that led to more questions, questions that Giorgio had set aside as submission and acceptance of being under control meant peace and survival.

Giorgio had responded with age old stories of right and wrong and win and lose. But how to tell his son that his Palestinian people lost to people who came with weapons and took away their freedom, telling them where they could and could not go. That is the real reason you cannot go to the sea. Anger rose as he wrestled with ways to explain their changed life that left only precious memories and broken dreams. "Why can't we go?" The boy's question begged a simple answer Giorgio could not give: the word occupation had little meaning for a youngster who knew no other kind of life. Soldiers with guns, checkpoints and travel controls were his normal life.

Giorgio accepted because he had to but his son's questions surfaced long suppressed thoughts. Despite promises of resolution, Israel's belief that 'The old will die off and the young will accept' supported continuing the occupation and prolonging resolution. He feared his son's quests and feared more a demand for his father to bring about justice. To stop his questioning meant accepting submission. At once annoyed he vowed to strive to make the boy change the history he could not.

His life and the freedom they knew before his son's birth were gone; normal for the young, imposed ignorance of the past. Occupation created new rules with restrictions and for Giorgio's boy relentless questions and a yearning to know the sea sparked his imagination.

Giorgio's thoughts of the time before his son's birth plagued him. Memories before blockades, checkpoints, gun wielding soldiers, home invasions, harassment and arrests – all came when the Palestine he knew became Israel, pushing native Palestinians out and forcing families to live as prisoners unable to move freely on their own land.

How, he wondered, *could he explain such historical complications to a child with right or wrong thinking? How can he accept wrong laws that* make it a crime to travel even to the next town and to the nearby Mediterranean Sea now in a new country that denies Palestinians to go to the sea?

Weapons ruled; and Palestine youngsters awakened in the early morning hours watch sleepily as soldiers sweep belongings from shelves, toss kitchen pots with food to the floor, stomp on clothes snatched from a drying line. All reminders that the prelude to a triumphant exit lets them know might rules, leaving distraught families to salvage, clean and put their home back together.

This is normal for my son, Giorgio thought; the past he and his wife remembered with gentle reflection and tears gone, guns ruled and his boy grows up witnessing Israeli soldiers yell and humiliate his father.

Only vivid imagination shapes his picture of the sea from his father's memory – water boundless as far as he could see touches the horizon at dark; and in morning brightness the sun bursts forth as a loud cry from the edge of darkness making a water painting in colors – black, purple red and orange, then golden sprinkled sparkles resting on a quiet face of calm like stars felled from the sky. Sounds like a dog drinking from a bottomless bowl make frothy white waves to greet a new day of expectation and hope. He pictured his Mama and Papa sitting at the water's edge looking at an endless sea stretching forever.

Giorgio feared the inevitable question for the pleasure pain it brought: *"Papa, why can't I know the sea?"* Tapping guilt, acquiescent acceptance, the eternal waiting with only hope and no action plagued him. Each question commanded understanding and required action the child could only feel as the insatiable question: *"Papa, why can't I know the sea?"* His plea for answers could no longer be ignored with evasion or passed off with unsatisfying answers. He determined to devote time and patience to direct his son toward fulfilling his longed-for dream of going to the sea. His mind captured by a thought: the arc of life is long but, in the end, it bends toward justice.

ESSAYS

The cure for anything is salt water: sweat,
tears or the sea.

ISAK DINESEN

First the Ferry,
Then the Skyway

BY BARBARA SARTOR
St. Petersburg, Florida

D id you ever ride a ferryboat? Don't you agree there's just nothing quite like it? Ferries give the traveler a chance to relax a bit, to slow down, and watch the water churning up behind, or rising up and making waves on the sides of the ships. Or, to watch the birds, drifting along as lazily as the clouds. They give passengers a pleasant break from driving with eyes glued to the road. A boat ride seems to bring out the friendliness in people too; they might even find themselves thinking quiet thoughts, in tune with the rhythm of the waves.

When I was a child in the 1930s, my dad worked with the Bee Line Ferry company in St. Petersburg, Florida. The ferries joined the outer edges of Tampa Bay, and shortened the trip from St. Petersburg to Sarasota by 49 miles—at least, that's what the signs claimed. Dad was captain of one of the boats, and we had many opportunities to go riding on them, usually just for fun.

I always enjoyed the crossings most when the wind was blowing and the boat was rolling a little. Once, I remember, a storm came up, and from the pilothouse we could see waves that appeared as high as the boat, though the boat was leaning to meet them, so they couldn't really have been that high.

The trip took about forty-five minutes each way, just long enough for passengers to take a little snooze, or a nice rest from driving. When dolphins were sighted, you could follow them with the eye for a long time, and they often came very near. Many other fish could be seen from the upper deck if one kept a sharp lookout.

And did you ever take time to watch a group of pelicans, often five or more, flying in formation? They glide along, flapping their wings to gain momentum, and then coast silently, searching for fish. Suddenly, one will break formation, hold his wings tightly to his sides, and zoom down with a splash to catch the unwary fish. Rarely do they miss. The boat was such a wonderful vantage point to watch their maneuvers. When the wind was fairly strong, the pelicans seemed to hang almost motionless in the air, still in formation, their great wings spread to keep them aloft.

Always there were the seagulls, roosting on the flagpole, or on the top deck; taking off periodically to practice a few dips, catch a fish, or to accept a few crumbs from a generous passenger. They were expert at catching thrown bits of food, and people who crossed frequently often brought snacks especially for the gulls.

If the captain happened to be your friend, you might be invited up to the pilothouse for a little visit; and if this captain happened to be Dad, you would almost certainly be invited to play a game of checkers. Dad became expert at the game with all this practice. He was pretty hard to beat. Forty-five minutes seems to be just about right to play one or two games, with a little conversation thrown in for good measure.

As the ferry neared Piney Point, on the Sarasota side, the captain would bid his guests good-bye, and take the wheel from the mate. From long experience he knew exactly how to line the boat up with the dock; taking into consideration the tide, winds, and current. Sometimes it appeared that we would surely crash against the guiding pilings, and it's true that we did bump them at times, but usually the landing was made quite effortlessly. The engines were kept going until lines had made the ship fast, and then the loading ramp was lowered onto her deck.

The cars, one by one, climbed the slight rise to the road. The interlude was over. Now—back to the business of passengers driving where they were going. But for the rest of their trip, I'm sure many of them appreciated the break in their driving, and looked back with pleasure to their ferryboat ride.

Today, the ferryboats are gone from Tampa Bay. Oh, one still makes regular runs, but just to carry sightseers around the waters there. The others have been sold or disposed of in other ways. In 1954, the first bridge opened and a second bridge was added in 1971. In 1980, tragedy struck when a ship hit the south bridge, collapsing it. Engineers then designed a six-lane, golden cable-stayed bridge in their place, built with concrete barriers to withstand the impact of huge ships.

Since 1987, the beautiful Sunshine Skyway bridge allows ships to pass under without delay on their way to Port Tampa. The high bridge has a magnificent view. As you drive up the height of the bridge, it is easy to imagine you are in an airplane, just flying low.

Now, I don't mean to imply that all the interesting things people saw from the ferryboat are gone just because a bridge has taken its place. The water is still there; the dolphins, the gulls, even the pelicans.

The planning for fill on the lower parts was wide enough to accommodate a few picnic parks. There are many places along the Skyway North and South fishing pier parks to fish or stop and look. The point is that many people will not take the time to stop and see things unless circumstances force them to. They just don't want to take the time. As a matter of fact, I believe there are more birds than ever, as the fishing piers make such an ideal resting place.

The reason for the bridge was plain enough. The ferries could not take care of all the traffic. At first there was only one ferry. Then two became necessary. Finally, even three boats were not able to take care of the increased traffic. Cars would have to stand in long lines for hours. I'm sure everyone has benefitted from the bridge. I'm also sure that some folks miss the ferries.

And Dad? In later years, he still ran a ferryboat. He captained boats crossing the Saint John's River, just south of Jacksonville, Florida. It was a nice trip, interesting with shrimp boats coming and going. The fishing was pretty good there too. Sometimes the air was filled with planes from the nearby Navy base zooming overhead. He didn't play checkers anymore though. The trip took exactly five minutes. Not enough time for a snooze, much less a game of checkers. I just might challenge my sons to a game of checkers next time they visit.

Barbara and Dad, "Captain Mac" McMullen

Photo: Sorenson Family

Proud Ferryboat Captain Mac McMullen, M.S. Sarasota,
St. Petersburg, Florida

Photo: Sorenson Family

Canoeing with Mom on the Juniper Springs Run

BY HENRY E. SORENSON, JR.
Juniper Springs in Ocala National Forest, Florida
Mom is Barbara Sartor of "First the Ferry, Then the Skyway"

I t didn't start well. When Ron and I arrived at the Juniper Springs Headwaters Facility, Ole and Brad were arguing in the parking lot. The gist of the altercation revolved around answering the critical questions, "Who had planned this trip and who should be in charge?" In other words, "Who was boss."

After they came to terms, we managed to check out and portage four canoes down to the loading dock— "we" being canoe tandem crews of Ron and Ole, Brad and Judy, Shaila and Julieta, and me and Mom. The Juniper Springs Run is a popular recreational destination—a nature-oriented, real Florida experience—not something concocted as artificial entertainment, with the carnival ride atmosphere for which Florida is so famous. Being so popular, there was some backup when we reached the dock, a line of impatient canoers waiting their turns to get in the water. A Park official was frantically directing the scene, making sure canoers kept the flow going and that no one cut ahead. When my turn came, I launched our canoe and pulled it around to the dock. Mom got in while I held the boat; then I got in and we were off. As soon as we were out of sight, I got out of the canoe and submerged myself in the crystal clear and bracingly cool water. The sun was bearing down. It was a hot day. Mom and I were either the last or next to last from our party to leave the dock. By the time we caught up to the others, they were all in the water cooling off too.

A series of thunderstorms had passed through earlier. There was debris from the storms scattering the landscape, including branches and downed trees—some that had fallen into the river creating obstacles along the route. Typically, Park personnel cut away such major obstacles in the river with chainsaws, but they hadn't had time to get to clearing before we were on the water. And the water was high and running fast.

For a while, all went well enough, nothing terribly eventful, just beautiful canoeing—picking our path through the winding, spring-fed stream under the canopy of shady oak trees—though the going was somewhat challenging all along because of the wreckage from the storms.

We were passed by some kayakers and occasionally another canoe, but mostly, we were more experienced than others on the river. We came upon and went around a number of family groups throughout the day. We passed a group of Asians when we were about halfway down the Run. When we reached the mid-point landing, we all took a breather. We pulled our canoes to the bank, jumped off the dock, and splashed around in the refreshing water to relax and cool down again before relaunching our canoes and paddling on.

A bit further on, Mom and I got into a running conversation with two brothers who were arguing with each other. The boy in the back of the canoe couldn't steer. The one in the bow couldn't go to the back because his brother was too large to be in the front. We ended up passing each other a few times at different obstacle areas on the river.

I noticed a thunderhead cloud forming above the canopy of trees and began to wonder if we might get rain. Mom and I were mostly on our own now as we didn't have much visual connection with others in our party. Ole and Ron were generally well ahead of us, though we would see them from time to time. I couldn't tell about the others—they were behind us somewhere. The overhanging brush and debris seemed to get more challenging the further we went.

About this time, we came upon a canoe manned by a red-headed teenage boy and his good buddy. They were sorry canoers—couldn't get their boat to turn. What they could do well was paddle fast and run into stuff—like trees, banks, and even other boats.

The sky turned dark. It started sprinkling. Then sprinkles turned to rain. Then came a full-on thunder and lightning storm. We were getting soaked as the thunder got closer and closer. Next thing we knew, it was right overhead and we were in the middle of it. Rain coming down in sheets, fierce thunder and lightning all around us. I was beginning to get seriously concerned for our safety. We were in a metal boat, on water, surrounded by tall trees. Not the best place to be in a raging electrical storm. I began looking for somewhere to pull over and get out. Ron and Ole had anchored themselves next to the bank by holding on to a tree branch. They seemed to be hanging on for dear life in the swift current. We pulled in next to them and held the canoes together like a pontoon bridge for Mom to get out. She made her way awkwardly, climbing from boat to boat and then onto shore and up the slippery bank.

Just then a humongous bolt of lightning struck a tall tree about ten feet away. BOOM! SPLAT! The tree fell across the river with a loud crash, spanking the water hard—right over the spot where our canoe would have been if we had kept on going. Branches and leaves were flying everywhere. We were shocked by the mighty display of sheer power and shaken by the simultaneous and deafening crack of thunder. I had never been so close to a lightning strike. I might have jumped out of my skin if such a thing were possible. Everybody scrambled out of the boats as fast as we could. We roped the canoes together with life vests and huddled under a low-canopied sable palm for protection from the rain. Ron held one of the great spreading palm leaves over Mom's head to ward off the deluge. We hunkered down and had a jolly time together under the palm fronds. We shared stories of old times—rain and lightning and thunder putting on a show around our little camp. A few other paddlers came by and had to work hard to get past the newly fallen tree, now almost fully blocking the river.

When the storm finally let up, we untied the boats and fought our way past the downed tree. We ran into the teenage boys again. The red-headed one was on the bank—no canoe, no paddle. The other was stranded just downstream. It was pretty obvious they knew nothing about canoeing, and they had headed out without any instruction. We found their boat ahead, trapped against one of those low hanging palms, its trunk almost touching the water. I managed to get the boat to the bank and in the hands of one of the boys. I think they had one paddle between them. Their parents came up and one of them gave an extra paddle to the boys. I almost said something but held my tongue. We wished them all luck.

In the faster running water, we constantly worked at negotiating the ever-winding path of the swollen watercourse and keeping our boat from running into fallen debris—a challenge to Mom's and my canoeing skills as we sped down the river. Mom was just a beginner.

We came up to another of those low hanging palms. A canoe ahead of us was fighting the current trying to make its way past. I tried to slow us as much as possible to give them time to get through and line us up so we could shoot the gap next to the bank. The other canoe took so long, I lost my line, and just as they cleared, we drifted out of position and towards the tree trunk. We might have been able to correct ourselves except right then the boys came flying down the river and pinned us to the tree. They flummoxed around for a while and had to get help from us, and their parents, to pull their canoe around the obstacle.

We were in a bad position, but I finally got us almost free... when we capsized. Mom leaned to one side to avoid a saw-edged palmetto petiole and over we went. Fortunately, the water was not deep at this point and the current was slow enough that I was able to get under the upside-down canoe, lift and drain it, and flip it over. Mom and I got back in, no worse for wear; we were already soaked through from the falling rain.

The river system opens up for the last third of the Juniper Run and instead of an overhanging canopy, the landscape turns to open marsh with reeds, grasses, and sandy beaches. Even though the river widened out here, there were still lots of obstacles. We were starting to get tired. It's a long trip even under the best of conditions—I believe about seven miles—and we were working hard.

Alligators like to bask along the banks in this sunny part of the Juniper Run. A girl had been killed and partially eaten by a gator just the week before in these same waters. She was out swimming in the river at around 5:00 p.m.—prime feeding time for alligators. I spied one good-sized gator, about seven or eight feet long, resting on the lip of the bank as we cruised by. It paid us no attention. It looked like it was made out of rubber, dark and glistening from the rain.

Our second capsize happened when we ran over a submerged tree trunk, parallel to our path, that lifted and flipped the boat as we went over it—a demonstration of just how fast the water was moving. Fortunately, we were far enough downstream that the basking alligator was no longer is sight. Mom ended up in deep, black muck alongside the bank. The bank was teeming with sawgrass and thorny blackberry bushes. I looked around, no alligators, so I pulled the canoe to shallower water—a bar in mid-stream. I tried to get Mom to me by extending a paddle to her to grab hold of. Her wet hair was plastered against her face, her feet were stuck in the mud, and she had lost a sandal. She discovered the blackberries and dined on a few. "These are really good!", she reported with remarkable cheer in her voice. Then, with concerted effort on both our parts, she managed to fight her way to the sandbar—all the while telling me about the struggle she was having getting across. Underwater grasses were clinging to her legs and holding on to her like in a horror movie.

When she got to me and was safely on the bar, I went to where she had been stuck in the mud and felt around for her sandal. No luck. I ate a few blackberries myself and picked some more for Mom—a token reward for our troubles. I crossed back over and tried my technique of getting under the upside-down canoe to lift and right it. Because of the depth of the river at this point, even on the bar, and the strength of the current, I wasn't able to completely lift the boat free of the water. I tried three times and was starting to give out.

Just then Shaila and Julietta cruised by. Shaila didn't even try not to laugh. As they passed us, she said Brad would be coming soon—he could help. Sure enough, he and Judy followed, right on cue. He and I righted the boat and steadied it while Mom climbed in.

Brad and Judy stayed within view from then on. Shortly before the end of the Run, the pilings of an old, long-gone bridge marched across the river. Mom and I steered between two sets of pilings like pros, but something happened to Brad and Judy and they had a jarring encounter with one of the columns.

There was a second, fully operational concrete bridge and roadway just ahead of the pullout and when we passed that, Ron and Ole were standing waste deep in the water, waiting to help guide Mom and me to shore. Shaila and Julieta arrived shortly thereafter, holding up Mom's missing sandal like a trophy. They had spied it floating down the river and snagged it. Amazing!

After pulling all the canoes out of the water, we arranged ourselves on wet towels in a circle on the grass. Ron and I opened a cooler and passed out sandwiches, juice, and beer that we had put together to enjoy at the end of the Run. Peanut butter and jelly never tasted so good.

The shuttle bus with its canoe rack arrived on schedule. Ole got into a tight moment, telling some other canoers to move their vehicle out of the way so the bus could get to the loading spot. They took their time, paying Ole no attention. One of them gave him the finger as they finally drove out. We lifted the canoes onto the racks and climbed into the shuttle bus. The Asian group we had met halfway down joined us— no sign of the teenage boys or their parents.

Back at the spring head, we unloaded the canoes, marking the end of the day's adventure. Chalk up another one for the record books. Next, we were off to Brad's house in Ocala for some barbeque.

Of course, there was one more bump in the road. Ron and I had to turn around at one point and drive all the way back to the canoe pickup point. In all the confusion, we had left his large, totally swamped beach towels on the ground.

That's about it—one memorable Juniper Springs Run—
with Mom.

Juniper Springs, Ocala National Forest, Florida

Photo: Henry Sorensen, Jr.

Bootprints From Yesteryear

BY RICK RHODES
Cedar Key, Florida

Cedar Key is northwest of Tampa on a part of Florida's Gulf Coast, often dubbed the Nature Coast. The area was once called 'Cedar Keys.' The Cedar Keys are a conglomeration of more than 30 islands. Most of the islands are quite small, but less than a half-dozen are sizeable enough to support a small population or a sawmill. Thirteen smaller, offshore islands comprise the 'Cedar Key National Wildlife Refuge (NWR).' The Cedar Key NWR provides safe habitat for a variety of wildlife, most notably wading and shore birds.

Today the general area is more commonly referred to as Cedar Key. Nearly all development in the Cedar Key area, as well as the town, is situated on the largest island of Way Key, accessible by road. Today's population of Cedar Key is estimated to be 700-to-800 permanent residents. However, it's the past two hundred years that form the eclectic towns of today.

Throughout its history, the Cedar Keys have hosted pirates, spies, blockade-runners and other assorted outcasts. During the early 1800s, Seahorse Key, one of the highest islands in the area, was reportedly used as a lookout post by French-speaking pirate Jean Lafitte. A few decades later, the key was an internment camp for Seminole Indians during the Second Seminole War. In 1854, Lieutenant George Meade (later General George Meade of Civil War fame) built the Seahorse Key lighthouse.

During the first half of the 19th Century the United States fought three wars with the Seminole Indians. Cedar Key was close to the action during the First, and especially the Second, Seminole War. In 1818, during the First Seminole War, General Andrew Jackson fought his way to Cedar Key, destroying Seminole property and lives. Near Cedar Key, Jackson encountered two British citizens whom he assumed were trading goods with the Indians. They probably were. Jackson soon had both summarily executed. Britain was so infuriated; she was about to go to war with the United States for the third time in 40 years. Congress, wishing to appease Britain, outwardly condemned Jackson. However, many tacitly approved, and Jackson was later elected our seventh U.S. President.

During the Second Seminole War (1835-42), Cedar Key was even more involved. In 1839, an Army depot and hospital were built on what was called Depot Key. That island was renamed Atsena Otie Key or 'Cedar Island' in the Native American tongue.

After the Second Seminole War, Cedar Key developed into an important port for the shipment of cotton, sugar, tobacco and lumber. The present town of Cedar Key was established on Way Key, the largest island. In 1853, the first Florida cross-state railroad was started. By 1861, this railroad connected the 155 miles between Way Key and Fernandina

Beach, on Florida's Atlantic Coast.

During the Civil War (1861-65), Cedar Key, like everywhere on the Southern Coastal States, was blockaded by Union troops. Thus, many locals became skilled blockade-runners. These Confederate blockade-runners carried cotton, turpentine, rosin, and lumber, and sneaked-in sugar, coffee, flour, sulfur, and gunpowder.

In those pre-refrigeration days, salt was a precious commodity. Salt was needed to preserve many foods. Wars were fought over salt. The effective Union blockade dried-up the pre-Civil War South's salt supply, previously imported from England. Hence, those resourceful Confederates began distilling their own salt from the waters of the Gulf of Mexico. When Union raiding parties attacked coastal settlements they knocked out as much Confederate salt production as possible by rupturing those huge cast-iron salt-water boiling kettles. By 1862, Union troops, coming from the Gulf, sacked Cedar Key again. This time Confederates abandoned the town.

After the Civil War, Cedar Key experienced rapid growth. The port and railroad were rebuilt. It became a major trading port with regular routes to New Orleans, Key West, and Havana, Cuba. By the 1880s, only the Florida ports Jacksonville, Key West, Fernandina Beach and Pensacola ranked ahead of Cedar Key. Sawmills, pencil mills, and a broom factory were built. The region's red cedar trees were ideal for splinter-free pencil stock. In 1888, the key's population peaked at 5,000.

By the dawn of the 20th Century, the red cedars were nearly depleted. Atop that, Florida entrepreneur and railroad man, Henry Plant selected Tampa over Cedar Key as his Florida's Gulf Coast rail terminus. That line was completed in 1884. If that wasn't bad enough, in 1896 a fierce hurricane, with over a 27-foot tidal surge, killed several hundred people, wiping out the existing railroad, pencil mills, and 5,000 square miles of standing timber. Cedar Key's heyday was over.

Today tourism is a substantial driver to the Cedar Key economy. This may have had its inception with noted environmentalist John Muir. Muir hiked 1,000 miles in seven weeks from Indianapolis to the Atlantic Ocean, and then southwestward across Florida to the Gulf of Mexico arriving at Cedar Key in 1867. When John Muir arrived in Cedar Key, the 29-year-old was sick with malaria and needed three months to recuperate. Muir was deeply impressed with Florida. Perhaps here in Cedar Key is where Muir first expressed his profundity: "that nature was valuable for its own sake...not only because it was useful for man." This principle guided Muir throughout the rest of his impactful life. After Muir departed the key, he eventually settled in California, where he helped establish Yosemite National Park (in 1882) and the Sierra Club.

Besides tourism, in the latter half of the 20th Century, the seafood industry heavily contributed to Cedar Key's economy. However, in 1994, the fishing net ban essentially put an end to large-scale commercial fishing. Nonetheless, sport fishing has remained popular. Every mid-October, the town hosts its annual seafood festival. In April, there's an art festival.

Restaurants, motels, bed and breakfasts, and boutiques

sprung up. Many upscale restaurants and boutiques are on Dock Street, the street closest to the Gulf. Many establishments on the southeastern side of Dock Street are built-out on pilings into the Gulf. A few of them have fallen victims in recent hurricanes. Cedar Key also has a hardware store, an auto parts store, a grocery store, and a handful of condos. Bird watching, bicycling, walking tours, and kayaking (on the calmer days) are popular.

The main part of town is about three blocks wide and about seven blocks long. Second Street parallels Dock Street. A few restaurants, motels, and other shops along Second Street may have non-waterfront prices. There is a small beach, with imported sand and a picnic pavilion, near the southeastern end of Second Street. The informative Cedar Key Historical Museum is located at the northwest corner of 2nd and D Streets. Visitors should note that D Street is the only road in and out of Cedar Key, and turns into Florida State Route 24 heading to the north-northeast.

Establishments along Dock Street, Cedar Key, Florida

Photo: Rick Rhodes

Peace of the Park

BY JOAN GIRARD BAPTIST
Safety Harbor, Florida

I
t was the spring of 1970, and four bell bottom-clad
friends cruised into Philippe Park in my boyfriend's '69
GTO. We picnicked, threw stones into the bay, laughed
and played the way teenagers do when they believe time is
endless and trouble free. To memorialize that carefree day,
I hopped on my boyfriend's shoulders, and he pretended to
hold up a tree by its mighty branch, while our companions
took photos of us.

That was the beginning of my life-long relationship with
that enchanting park. It is a simple county park, but very special
to both ancient and current-day residents. It is situated in
Safety Harbor on a bluff overlooking the upper end of Tampa
Bay. The park's namesake is Odet Philippe, who was the first
non-native settler in Pinellas County. He arrived in 1842, and
he is credited with introducing grapefruit to Florida. The park
is on land that was once part of the Philippe plantation. Long
before Philippe arrived, the park was home to the Tocobaga
people. Their temple mound is in the park, for which the park
is designated a National Historic Landmark.

Since that day in 1970, the park has been my go-to place.
In my community college years, it was my study hall. During

my 5K years, it was my practice track. My family and friends held an untold number of picnics, baby showers, and birthday parties under its shelters. In my younger years, I shared sweet kisses with boyfriends du jour by its waters. Year after year, I witnessed the Great Horned Owls raise their chicks in the safety of one of the park's ancient oak trees. On occasion I spotted a manatee or bald eagle. I have found countless painted rocks in the park, kept them for a while, and then released them back to the park for someone else to discover.

My dog, Alex, loved walking in the park. Her tail would start wagging excitedly and she would begin her happy bark as soon as we approached the park's entrance. In her puppy years, I could hardly keep up with her trotting along the seawall. In her senior years, there was lots of shade and resting places for her. At the playground, children would flock to Alex, and she would gently accommodate their gleeful squealing and petting.

During my husband's last year of life, I often took him to the park to absorb the serenity and calm. The park was a special place for my mom and me during her final years. We would set our chairs by the water, relax in the soft breeze, listen to the softly lapping waves, and just be together.

These days, when I feel the weight of the world on my shoulders, I go to the park and breathe in the salt air and peace. I visit the same tree from the picture, which still stands with its long low branch sweeping over the bay waters. And I remember that I am not carrying the weight alone. Like that spring day in 1970, I am on the supportive shoulders of all my loved ones who have shared the peace of the park with me.

Sunset Reflections, Clearwater, Florida

Photo: Suzanne Norman

A Nostalgic Night at the Blueberry Patch

BY KENDEL OHLROGGE
Gulfport, Florida

The Blueberry Patch is definitely the place to go for retired hippies. With its promise of a peace-loving community, creative types like me can't possibly be found elsewhere. My late great friend Aldo Moroni introduced me to the place, one unlike any other I had ever seen. Founder Dallas Bohrer first saw it back in 1977 as a reprieve for peace-loving artists, writers, musicians and performers. He pictured them coming together, using their creativity to entertain the people of Gulfport regularly each month.

Bohrer's dream steadily gained popularity, yet it was only after his death, when it eased into a 501(c)(3) charitable organization, that it achieved the height of its popularity. Today, four decades later, it continues to grow and gain award achievements of local and outside standing. Among these awards is the prestigious Best Public Artwork, which shares center stage with the Salvador Dali Museum as first runner-up and puts Gulfport forefront as a major attraction. Yep, gotta love Gulfport.

I'd been to Blueberry Patch a couple of years ago with my friend Aldo, who knew about artwork from work he had commissioned on an art piece there. Tonight, I returned by myself for the pot luck open-mic jam yet feeling alone and very much out of place. I wasn't sure of what time things got started or even what "pot luck" meant. Do I bring food to share? Or if sold there, maybe there was no guarantee about the quality of the food. Somewhat familiar with artsy types, I wondered if marijuana would be available and passed around. I came empty-handed and feeling hungry, I thought at least there'd be someone selling hot dogs or tacos.

Still, I found Blueberry to be a kind of magical fantasy place that likely lived up to founder Bohrer's vision as an array of outdoor art studios, each with its distinctive artistic mark and unique flare. The exhibits are complimented by the street events with tourists, locals and artists bonding to share enjoyment.

I was driven to join in too, glad I had come an hour early despite feeling out of place, lost and hungry. A booth that sold vegan smoothies and burgers had opened, manned by a thin man wearing a turban and eye patch, I ordered a smoothie and burger. Intrigued by his efficiency, I was captivated watching him as I sipped the refreshing banana-strawberry smoothie he had prepared before flipping my burger onto the grill deftly using a soup ladle. He gave me a choice between a homemade sesame seed, rosemary or plain bun. I chose sesame seed but, unaccustomed and puzzled, can't say why. I watched fascinated, as a big splash of mustard spewed forth covering the entire bun. He asked if I wanted lettuce too. I nodded. Finally, he handed me the burger, almost entirely obliterated by a generous salad topping. Maybe it was hunger, but I remember it as being the most enjoyable burger I ever tasted.

I'd read that a recent scientific study found tests had proven that each hot dog eaten costs thirty-three minutes of life. True or not, I decided that even though the burger could have used less mustard, I was NOT going to become a vegan.

Like many places I've been and loved visiting—while not my lifestyle—I appreciate the alternate styles that are out there. Life would be dull without them.

The Blueberry Patch, Gulfport, Florida

Photo: Kendel Ohlrogge

Coastal History at Weedon Island Preserve

BY LOUISE S. HARRIS
St. Petersburg, Florida

When I think of the Tampa Bay region, what comes to mind are blue skies, sunny beaches, year-round water sports and picnics, and a land blessed with a variety of sparkling water views. Hiking in the Weedon Island Preserve, I discovered that this region is also home to a treasure trove of hidden gems.

The Weedon Island Preserve, listed on the National Register of Historic Places, offers a way to experience Florida wildlife from the vantage point of sturdy boardwalks, a peaceful canoe or kayak adventure and trails through woodlands teeming with wildlife nestled in a protected area between the cities of Tampa and St. Petersburg. I took a hike to explore part of this preserve's 3,200 acres, and I encourage other nature lovers to do the same.

My first stop was the education center for a little help preparing my hike. The education center staff provided a backpack filled with a variety of activities and field guides. Classes, discussions and lectures for visitors are also offered there. Although I did not have time to take a class or listen to a lecture that day, I read the information on my own and noted upcoming classes of interest on my calendar. I appreciated the insights into coastal Florida wildlife such as the behaviors of wading and water birds like roseate spoonbills, herons and others along with the birds of prey in the sky, those majestic ospreys, hawks, and bald eagles.

As I sat on a bench to read and plan my path, a screech from the sky startled me. The shadow of a large osprey overhead caught my eye, and I decided to accept that grand bird's invitation to follow its direction. I jumped up, stuffed my hiking guide in the backpack and hurried to catch up before losing sight of the osprey that was casually cruising the sky above the treetops.

The osprey's flight led me to the 200-foot fishing pier, which stands near the location of the historical bridge that once connected Weedon Island with neighboring Snell Island to the south. It is a popular spot to cast a line and wait for sheepshead, jack, snook and other fish to bite. In awe, I watched the prowess of the osprey. I witnessed its vertical plunge into the sunlit water with such precision, to capture a fish. When the osprey circled back up into the sky to perch briefly on a high branch, I was thrilled to capture its handsome portrait. I watched that osprey fly away with the silver fish in its beak, perhaps to share with a family waiting for lunch in their hidden nest. I figured that osprey and I both got our "catch of the day."

Next, I traversed the trail to the 1,100-year-old canoe that archaeologists discovered in Pinellas County. Although the canoe was found in 2001, the team excavated the site in 2011, revealing a canoe nearly 40 feet long from bow to broken stern. The Weedon Island canoe is far longer than any other dugout found in Florida and is associated with the goal of use in a saltwater environment. The makers of the canoe are considered to belong to the Manasota culture, a tribe who hunted and fished the bay, leaving shell mounds along the coast.

Paddlers can bring canoes, kayaks or paddleboards and they can rent what they need at the preserve. The self-guided paddling trail is a 4-mile loop, with a canoe/kayak launch site. Gliding along the bay waters where birds swoop and mullets leap, it is easy to imagine the action in and around the water that ancient Manasota paddlers traversed on their daily excursions.

The mangrove and coastal hammock preserve provides habitats for more than fish. Protected gopher tortoises and their burrows are found along these trails. There are plenty of boardwalks to meander and experience the beauty of the preserve, the glistening water and big sky. To increase accessibility for all, there are almost two miles of handicap-accessible boardwalks and pavement that is available to visitors using wheelchairs and strollers. Boardwalks extend through tidal flats, lush mangrove habitats and saltwater ponds teeming with mullet and wading birds.

Along the west boardwalk loop stands a 45-foot observation tower where guests enjoy a stunning vista of the preserve, Tampa Bay, and the cities of St. Petersburg and Tampa. The flight momentum of the snowy egrets, great blue herons, and other beautiful birds energized me as I walked, enjoying the bay breeze. Hiking through the Weedon Island Preserve is a peaceful adventure and a unique opportunity to walk the ancient paths of the Manasota people.

Catch of the Day

Photo: Carlene Cobb

ABOUT
THE CONTRIBUTORS

Joan Girard Baptist has lived in the Tampa Bay area for most of her life. During her eight years living in Atlanta, she attended Southern Polytechnic State University to take classes specializing in usability and technical writing and communication, after which she graduated from Dekalb Technical Institute. Among her many careers Joan was in the technical communication profession for over 20 years, crafting online help, user guides, and procedural manuals, as well as managing and mentoring writers. Now retired, she lives in Clearwater, Florida and has the time to explore and develop her creative writing skills.

Carlene Cobb grew up in south Tampa, inspired by the sea and Florida's amazing, colorful skies. After winning an award in a short story contest hosted by University of South Florida, College of Arts and Letters, she was encouraged by writing professors and other mentors to write fiction, which she continued to do. Another important goal was to be a self-supporting writer, working as a communications director, staff writer, managing editor, and contracted correspondent. Her first nonfiction book was traditionally published by Rosen Publishing Group, NY. Her stories have been published in *TIME*, *Arts Coast Magazine*, *Tampa Bay Metro Magazine*, *Tampa Magazine*, *Tampa Bay's Best Magazines*, *St. Petersburg Times*, *The Tampa Tribune*, *Florida Health Care News* and other print and online publications. Today her first novel is in progress. Her short stories, Seaside Gardener and Cottage 15 appear in this collection, offering a prelude to her debut novel.

Louise Harris grew up in Drexel Hill, Pennsylvania and Cape May, New Jersey. She went to the University of Maryland College of Journalism. She became an editor and has worked on newsletters, wire services, radio copy, online publications and clients' manuscripts. She has authored four romance novels, the most recent being released in October 2023; one children's chapter book; and a nonfiction book on addiction with another author. She also ghostwrote two cookbooks with a local chef. She has lived in St. Petersburg, Florida since 2013.

Suzanne Mehrtens Norman is a native of Charleston, South Carolina. She grew up exploring the Lowcountry marshes, rivers and beaches. At age 20, she moved to Clearwater, Florida, studied at St. Petersburg College, and earned a Master Writer Certificate from the Society for Technical Communication. Her 28+ years as a professional award-winning writer includes work at corporations, newspapers and magazines. Writing specialties include web content, arts, travel, and nature nonfiction articles published in *Arts Coast Magazine, Canoe & Kayak, St. Petersburg Times,* and others. Coastal Voices and Visions is her first fiction publication. She lives on the Gulf coast in Dunedin, Florida.

Doris F. Norrito is a native of Long Island, New York. In 1990, she moved to Florida where she actively pursued her writing career as an independent journalist. As a world traveler, she visited most of North and South America, Europe, Asia, and the Middle East. Her published work has appeared in *St Petersburg Times, Tampa Bay Newspapers, Pinellas News "Our Heritage" columnist, Tampa Bay Business Journal, Florida Living,* and *Christian Social Action.* She also worked for International Middle East Media Center on reportage from Palestine/Israel in Bethlehem and WMNF Community Radio volunteer news broadcaster. She enjoys watching wild birds from her home in Seminole, Florida on the Gulf coast.

Sadly, Doris Norrito passed away in 2023. She was an astute editor, helping to assemble this spirited collection of stories and essays. Doris was a beloved mother, grandmother, and treasured friend who will be sorely missed.

Kendel Ohlrogge was raised in Zumbrota, Minnesota. He earned a Juris Doctorate in Law at the University of Minnesota Law school and practiced in Minneapolis for many years. Now semi-retired, he writes children's books, poetry, published reviews of travel and businesses, and the upbeatoffbeat.blog highlighting everyday life's idiosyncrasies. His children's book "Oh No! Where do Kites Go?" can be found on Amazon. He lives on the Gulf coast in Treasure Island, Florida.

Captain Rick Rhodes has researched and authored ten nonfiction books, including "Cruising Guide to Florida's Big Bend Coast," by Pelican Publishing Company and where much of his Cedar Key information comes from. In 2019, he authored "Post-Hurricane Michael Assessments, Cruising Guide to Florida's Big Bend–From Steinhatchee to Panama City, Florida". The guide includes "A History of Gulf Coast Hurricanes". His latest book is: "They Made America Great –31 Endearing Legacies Worth Heeding Today" available at www.rickrhodes.com. A former US Army Corp of Engineers instructor and Peace Corps veteran, he lives in St. Petersburg, Florida along the Gulf coast.

Barbara Sartor grew up in St. Petersburg, Florida. Her father, Early Jackson McMullen, and his family were early settlers ("Crackers") of Pinellas County. Barbara studied at St. Petersburg College and University of South Florida, Tampa, where she earned a Master's degree. She is a retired guidance counselor. As a military wife and mother of four sons, she lived in Japan, Alaska and other US bases. Her published work has appeared in the *Christian Science Monitor* and *St. Petersburg Times*. She lives on the Gulf coast in Dunedin, Florida.

After 100 years of vibrant life, Barbara passed away in 2024. She was a cherished mom, grandmother, and friend who loved her family adventures. It is an honor to include her memorable ferry boat essay which will touch the hearts of readers.

Henry E. Sorenson, Jr. (Hank) is Professor Emeritus of Architecture on the faculty of Montana State University. In 1983, he came to Montana from his native Florida after earning a Masters of Architecture degree at University of Florida. He developed a series of architectural graphics courses for the M.S.U. School of Architecture. It was a golden opportunity; one for which he had been preparing all his life, as he always excelled in drawing.

An avid outdoorsman, Hank enjoys exploring and has traveled extensively in the Americas, Europe and Asia. He is the son of Barbara Sartor who is also featured in this collection. When he is at home in Bozeman, it is said that those passing by his house in the early evening are often treated to the melodic strains of live, acoustic guitar music emanating from within.

Sadly, Henry passed away in 2023. He was a beloved son, husband, father, brother and friend who will be missed by all. He was a true talent in the artistic endeavors he pursued. We thank him for his canoe adventure essay and beautiful photography contributions to this collection.

ACKNOWLEDGMENTS

Thanks to the editors and fellow writers in St. Petersburg, Pinellas County and the greater Tampa Bay area. We appreciate this supportive, creative community, especially members of the former Bay Area Professional Writers Guild. Your publications inspired us to compile this collection.

We are also grateful to professors at the University of South Florida and St. Petersburg College for their encouragement. And, we thank the *Tampa Bay Times* team, sponsor of the annual Festival of Reading/literary event, for bringing many varied authors and readers together over the years.

REFERENCES

The following places were visited for research for this collection:

- St. Petersburg Museum of History in St. Petersburg, Florida

- Weedon Island Coastal Preserve in St. Petersburg, Florida

The following books were used to confirm facts:

- Cobb, Ashton. *Kiawah Island, A History*, Charleston: The History Press 2006

- DeYoung, Bill. *Vintage St. Pete, The Golden Age of Tourism and More*, St. Petersburg: St. Petersburg Press 2020

- Rhodes, Captain Rick, *Cruising Guide to Florida's Big Bend*, New Orleans: Pelican Publishing; 2003

Printed in the USA
CPSIA information can be obtained
at www.ICGtesting.com
LVHW050455291124
797894LV00045B/1242